The Therapist

and

Other Stories

Lynley Barnett

A catalogue record for this
book is available from the
National Library of Australia

Linellen Press
265 Boomerang Road
Oldbury, Western Australia
www.linellenpress.com.au

Dedication

To all those who have helped me in my writing life.

Other titles by Lynley Barnett

Letters from Nanna
The Spectacular Cat
Sophie's Story
Peter's Story
Zac's Story
Tommas's Story
Tips from a Mediator

Contents

The Therapist

You may think you know all about therapy, what it's like to be 'In' therapy, what it's like to be able to say whatever you wish without having to catch each word, to watch every sentence and make sure you do not trip yourself up with your words.

But you don't.

Therapy is more than just talking. It's cleaning, comforting, and warming. Sometimes, it takes my breath away. Sometimes, it feels like being held, for that moment, as an interesting person, as a person who could be loved.

Therapy is listening, I think, and the listening is special. Listening is a word that needs explaining. Being listened to is not just being able to repeat my words; it's being able to understand *my* words and knowing why I chose those words. Because those are the words that are going to tell you why I did what I did and who I am.

The world sees only what I did, and judges me. But in Therapy what I did has a place surrounded by words. And there is understanding. And in that understanding there is a kind of togetherness, that's what I call it. I cannot tell you how special that is; it's like a comfort, a support, and an okayness for me to be me and to speak without the need to blame myself.

I am here because the courts have dictated that I must be here, but I am here because I want to be here. I want someone to know what my life was like and why I made the most terrible decisions.

I am talking into my tape recorder because my writing is not good. But my Therapist, Elizabeth, has given me this so I can tell you today what it is like to be me. She said I can start anywhere.

So I want to say I don't want to be in gaol, not even this Children's Gaol. I would have done anything not to be here. Gaol is a cold, old place. Old buildings, old rooms, old beds. Everything is old. Everything is cold. There is little comfort, there is only sameness, and every day is the same. The scared looks the other prisoners give me as I walk through the common room towards my cell … that doesn't change either. I leave them with their fantasies, that way they leave me alone. But I want the therapy the courts have given me. I want the space that allows me to really be myself. The space in which I can say this is me, this is what I did, and this is why I did it.

You see, in that small piece of time, I am heard.

I know that much of what I say will end up in a report on a judge's table. I can live with that. Why? Because there is an understanding between myself and Elizabeth that when I talk freely, she will hear the real me, and she will not expose this me in words on paper. She will not give it to a stranger whose skills are not the same as hers. She has the skills of warmth and tenderness. She tells me this is what she calls empathy. The stranger will judge me, and I will have to live with that – oh, did I say that? No, maybe the stranger will judge me and I will have to die because of it.

But either way, I will have had the satisfaction of knowing that in this world, I am heard.

Therapy is like that. Even the room Elizabeth sits in has a feeling of comfort. Of wrapping you up in a blanket of understanding, and the heart beat I hear that cannot be described is the heart beat of being me.

I have told Elizabeth of the endless nights of lying in terror. I cannot remember a day or a night when I was not fearful. And that is another word that is not understood. To be fearful is to be full of fear. Can you even imagine a child whose every waking moment is full of fear? No, you cannot. Well, I lived those fearful days and the terror-filled nights. The times when I could not see what was coming next. The hand, the belt, the language that caused my soul to shrivel. Did you know souls can shrivel? Elizabeth knows that, and she allowed me to draw my shrivelled soul. I drew one tiny pinprick of red on the large canvas sheet she gave me. That is shrivelled. But you have never been there, have you.

There is a never-endingness about fear: it is around every corner, behind every door, and in places that live only in my imagination. It is everywhere, like the air that you breathe, only here's the crazy part: it isn't like the air you breathe. It's like there is no air to breathe. And that causes pain in my chest because I cannot breathe. Only after the hand has fallen or the belt has hit me is there relief until the next time, and while I wait for the next time, the fear starts to build up again.

I think of it as a moving bicycle; how else can I explain the wheel that keeps turning and never stops but only slows down? That is fear. So when I say I am fearful, you know that this is more than a road under the wheels of your car or a sky above you; it just never stops.

And pain. Do you think you know pain? Well, you don't know pain. You know the absence of pain because you are well, all I know is pain. There is pain in my head and pain in my body. I have learned to control the pain in my body. I have found a switch that seems to lessen the pain almost like turning myself into nothingness, but the pain in my head is beyond bearing, and that is my downfall. Because I scream with that pain, and when I do that, the belt falls again, and the boot crushes me, and I seem to have no control over that pain.

Elizabeth is making me play small games where I am allowed

to scream for one minute – never more than one minute – and instead of a boot, I get a warm blanket around me. I think sometimes she holds me too, although sometimes I am not aware of what she is doing. I always feel so different after that exercise. I think she is letting me get rid of all my screams until I will have no more screams left. And I think that is such a clever idea. Although I see at the end of my scream time she has tears in her eyes, and I wonder at that. Why don't I have any tears in my eyes?

She talks about making my soul grow again. And I don't know if I can believe that but she will have some clever idea to share with me about that. I said share. She shares things. I have never had anyone who has shared anything with me. I have always been the lost boy, the left-to-one-side boy, the never-picked-sports boy. I thought it was me, and she said, yes, it probably was me; I scared people away. But she is not scared of me and I think she has ways to show me how I can be different. I don't know how to be different, but she does.

You see that is what Elizabeth does. She doesn't just do words, she teaches me. And she has done something else for me … she has made a time for me for every day. I have MY time every day. Do you know how that feels? There is someone who wants to listen to me every day – well, every day except for Saturday and Sunday, and on those days she gives me games to play. I miss her, but I do as she asks.

I don't know how long she will be my therapist. Is there a length of time she is allowed to be someone's therapist? I shall have to ask her that. And when I said that, I felt terribly fearful. I have to stop the fear by drawing, as she has taught me, or by imagining my favourite place on the beach, sitting in the sun, as she has taught me.

I do wonder if she will be able to explain to the Judge that when I killed my stepfather, I knew what I was doing. I did. I truly did. Like a dog deliberately run over by a car and left for dead. I meant to leave him dead. I could not find any other way of making sure he could not raise his hand to me again. I wasn't thinking about anyone else, just me. I wanted there to be some peace in my head. I wanted the pain to go away.

He kept his car tools in the shed out the back and I knew what a wrench could do. He broke my arm with that last year, but he told the hospital that I fell down the steps, and they believed him. I didn't kill him when he was angry; no, he had far too much strength for me. I am tall but thin for my age but that might have something to do with what I am allowed to eat. If there is a chore left undone, I don't get dinner. It's always been that way, even long before my Mum died, and that was so many years ago now – I have forgotten how old I was.

No, I waited until he was asleep. Yes, I planned it. The police asked me that. So I told them, of course, I planned it; it was when he was asleep, or I would be thrown down the back steps and belted for waking him. He didn't wake, and yes, I did hit him more than once. I knew he would get up if I only hit him once.

The police asked me if I felt sorry for what I had done, and I didn't lie. I seem to remember my mother telling me I mustn't lie. So I told them the truth: my heart almost stopped when I did it, and then I felt nothing. Just glad he couldn't do it anymore. They asked me what "it" was, and I didn't know if they were serious or not so I showed them the belt and buckle marks on my back. That's when they stopped asking me questions.

And that's how I met Elizabeth, my therapist. In my eyes, she is beautiful. Her hair is grey and moves around her face when she talks. She is as tall as I am, but not as thin as me, and she has these soft blue eyes. Mine are green. She dresses in such comfortable clothes, but they always seem to match her eyes.

She explained what a therapist was, and she tells me that I

have to stay in gaol until she has finished her report. And I can tell when she says that, that she is sad. But I don't mind. I get to see her from Monday and every weekday and like I said earlier therapy is more than just talking. Sometimes it takes my breath away. Sometimes it is quiet time, sometimes drawing time, but always it is time with a person like Elizabeth who sneaks a tear when I talk. And I see it roll down her cheeks. And it is someone who lets me sneak a hug before she goes.

And I wonder, is this what my mother might have done if she had stayed alive?

☙

I wrote
a tiny tale
put it somewhere
lost it.

☙

(Tiny Tales are only ten words long — try writing one.)

A Skeleton in the Cupboard

The bones were intact, and the feathers too, all nestled in a carved box and kept in his cupboard.

The box was not so very big. Well, there aren't too many bones in a little bird, are there?

Yet he kept the box as a reminder of the faithful bird who had whistled him awake each day and who had reminded him each evening that, when the sun went down, it was time to cease the busyness of the day and enjoy the peace and quiet. He needed those reminders because he wasn't very good at organising his day into anything that had time structures.

In fact, he spent most of his day in semi-darkness, his computer humming as his fingers sped over the keys. And sometimes he had mistaken night for day and day for night. That was until he'd been given the small parrot – the parrot that lived in a resplendent cage on his balcony and became raucous after the sun came up. Her squawk alerted the man to the beginning of the day, and he watched the arrival of the birds that came to clean up the spilt seed that his bird dropped. He taught it how to whistle. And he marvelled at its ability to imitate him. He laughed at its off-key notes and wondered if his whistling was as unmusical as the bird portrayed.

When he needed to stretch his legs, he would wander out to the bird and engage it in conversation, none of which made any sense to the bird, but which still gave him the comfort of some company.

He had called the bird Peggy, because he thought she was female, well that seemed to be the case. He had read online the signs to look for in a female, and yes she had all those markings. She seemed to know her name. She inclined her head when he spoke her, almost as though she was responding to his call. And when he talked to her, she imitated his mouth opening and shutting, but without sound. She came into her own when he whistled "Row, row, row your boat, gently down the stream," and would join in with her version of the song.

She gave him pleasure and company. Who would have thought it. A small bird, a member of the parrot family, who seemed to enjoy his company every bit as much as he enjoyed hers. She would come to his hand and sit on it, and when flying in the Lounge room, she spent more time flying back to him than flying to the curtains or the sofa. She would look for his gold chain, to play with, and tugged at anything shiny he might be wearing.

And then, one day, she was no longer. Just a wee bird at the bottom of the cage. And a man with a broken heart placed her into a box as he tried to start his day without the familiar wake-up call. And he wondered how he had ever managed without her, and then sadly, who would care about him in the future?

CR

A Story for Our Times

Yellow shirts flying, leg muscles tiring they came. 5,6,7,8 cycle riders around the corner and down the Cycleway.

This was supposed to be the way to approach later life activities, the way to keep up with the gossip, the politics, the personal problems, listen to the advocates of welfare, betting tips, cycle maintenance, caravan conundrums – this my friends was supposed to be *the* life.

How to manage older age and retirement and get the most out of every day. How to stay positive and active and live every moment to its fullest. This was the example to set for future retirees: not how to get ready for death, but how to transition to life, how to live again. Anyway, that's what she'd read.

To find the wind in your face, the chill around your ears, the spark from your helmet that sends the magpies crazy, the scope of your vision taking in nature's beauty and man's wreckage …

Aaah, this was what you might have been waiting for. But not her. She struggled to keep up with the group. Number seven, with tail-end Charlie behind her. Eight in this group, pedalling as though their life depended upon it, so she followed suit. Harder, faster, de-seated over a stone, reclaiming her seat with a gasp. Onward, onward.

So what had persuaded her to join the Over 55's Cycle club? The company, the fellowship, having something interesting in her life that made her get up each day? Nothing of the kind.

Yes, all her reasons seemed as true for her today as they had been last month. She grimaced when her pedal slipped and grazed her ankle. Her intent in joining the Club was really so different to the group's expectations.

She had long harboured a desire to allow revenge to be hers. She had long harboured a desire to take back the wasted years, to triumph over the adversity of her past.

Six years she had spent in prison. Six years to formulate a plan, a smart, intelligent appraisal of her giftedness, and her ability to wait until the time was right. Now the stars were in alignment, and her waiting and planning were over.

The group came to a stop at the "A" Shed. Refreshments beckoned; a meeting place to rebuild the stamina a little, to refuel on the coffee-high needed. And she thought as she adjusted the helmet, carefully taking it from her head so not to move the mousey brown wig and the dark bland glasses she wore, that this was indeed her time.

She watched where he sat, his loud laugh preceding him, then as he walked up to order his coffee she calmly walked over to "order" her own coffee. And she waited until they had both been served. As his coffee came out and his conversation continued in the direction of his table, she just slipped the tablet into his coffee. It had no taste or smell, nothing to alert him, and she turned and went to the table behind him to sit, and wait.

He took his coffee. And he drank his coffee at his table, still regaling his companions with his prowess in everything, and she watched as his face changed, and he slid to the floor in convulsions.

Her job was done. Those lonely years in prison working in the library, a trusted prisoner, had given her access to all the information in the world. It really wasn't so difficult to access the materials needed and the internet provided the perfect recipe.

Now all that remained was to quietly disappear. The false name she had used to join the club would lead to nowhere.

She had her plans in place, a little rest in the country, and when he was forgotten, she would move on. She had acquired so many skills in prison – finding work after COVID would be easy. He had made his money using her giftedness, and had hung her out to dry when confronted over the large government money theft. So, this was simply Au Revoir; she had repaid him, she said to herself, "in spades".

You just don't take a woman's giftedness for granted unless you have a death wish, do you?

ॐ

Acrostic

A
T iny
A nd
L oving
E ndeavour
F rom
O ne
R ather
O verworked
U nderpaid
R esearch
T utor
I s
M aking
E mployers
S ing

What was the endeavor, you ask?
To be continued next week.

☙

An Extra Ordinary Relative

During the hard times of the Second World War, many heroic tales emerged. Almost every family found within it a member who did something special, who went above and beyond the call to duty. Many of their deeds were quietly done and very rarely spoken about.

Sometimes, it was not until their funeral that family members understood that they had walked beside an "extraordinary relative".

My grandfather was one of those men.

He was too old to go to war. Instead, he lived a life behind the scenes in New Zealand.

He saw the young men who left New Zealand's shores, who left behind wives and families. And he found a way to keep the families who were left behind safe and fed.

He accepted every piece of jewellery the wives and womenfolk offered him and gave them cash for food and other necessities. The jewellery was sometimes valueless, but he put a value on it. He paid them whatever they thought it was worth, and he promised to keep it until the end of the war when it could be "bought back" and worn again.

He allowed the families to maintain their pride and their ability to provide for their children, and he did this without mention to others.

But word had a way of getting around, and the small city he lived in knew they had a "bank" they could rely on when things got tough. Many items were redeemed and pawned time and time again.

He never refused to find the money for them. He never asked questions. This was an honour system: he paid for the item, and held it in trust until it could be bought back.

Wedding rings were just stock in trade, here today and bought back tomorrow when the soldier returned from leave. Sometimes they could be lent back for the soldiers leave, if he was not supposed to know of the hardships at home. There must have been many a woman who "Lost" a brooch and found it again at the end of the war.

And I have always wondered how he managed to find the cash from his little jewellers shop to continue to do this throughout the war.

At the end of the war, he had a few items that were never "bought back", their owners had died and there was no one to return the ring or the brooch to.

My mother was given two rings and she wore them in memory of my grandfather. I asked her about them one day, and she told me the story I have written.

My grandfather was a gentle, kind, and wise man. I knew him for just a little while as a child. He had the qualities of a real diamond, brilliantly cut and giving of joy.

May he rest with the families he fed and clothed during the hard times of World War Two.

☙

Behind the Doors of a Psychiatric Unit

During the course of one year, in most Western Societies, Psychiatric Units can shine a significant light on what is happening in a community.

The weekend when the Taylor Swift concerts were on is the first of many examples. Admitted into the hospitals will be one or perhaps two Taylor Swifts. They're having a psychotic episode often brought on by a fruit salad of drugs. But sometimes it is the breakdown of their personalities.

For the drug takers, it is 48 hours or longer that they will wear the persona of Taylor Swift. Those whose personalities are fragile may stay in the persona for longer. But it isn't only the girls who take a trip into an unreal world of their own making. The wards will sport an Elvis, when the Elvis Show is in town or a Buble when the Buble name goes up in lights, and then the replica arrives at the hospital doors. The strangest of these adopted personalities was the patient who, many years ago, purported to be the Spice Girls. There were five Spice Girls so the personas of the deluded woman became quite muddled.

Over the years, Elvis's personality has invaded many men. When there appeared to be a revival of his music, his personality would walk through the hospital doors escorted by the police, or members of the patient's family. The Beatles all had their replicas in one or other Psychiatric Unit many times over their public life time. And in the modern world only the names of the stars have changed.

Delusions are not only the outlet of the very ill; they are also adopted by many a neighbour or friend, but the difference is that while we all live with our projections and deeply held ideas, we can also usually live in the real world. The delusions are minor, they do not greatly affect anyone's daily life. If you always hang the clothes on the line with a his followed by a hers article, it only matters to the washer of the clothes. But those who adopt an 'other' self and get totally immersed to the exclusion of reality, often in that other personality, become a danger to themselves or to others. So, too, do those who have insistent voices controlling their lives.

Many people walk a fine line between staying in the world and falling into a completely unreal world, as many plastic surgeons can attest.

I want to look like … … Please change my face, my waist, my bottom, my ears, my jaw … whatever the body part is that they think requires adaptation, in the patient's view. Successive operations occur because one operation is never enough. One change requires a second change and then a third.

There are those who want to look like an animal – a tiger, a leopard – and surgery is their choice to create the look they want. They usually remain outside hospital walls because they can continue living some part of their lives in reality. They get the term of 'eccentric' applied to them, and they get the attention they seek.

Reality is a term we apply to those who live and work in the world, who are capable of adhering to the rules of the community, and who understand rules and can apply them to themselves.

But good Mental Health can be a difficult task to maintain for many. There are those who are resilient, and adaptable. Those whose circumstances have given them protection while they were growing up, those who accepted the advice or the wisdom needed to overcome hurdles. And then there are those who live in a fragile world without much resilience to combat what life throws at them. Those who have little in their world to give them support. And the third group is those who have been strong and capable all their lives and who get a succession of unrelated horrors happening around them. These are all of us who may succumb to accidents and incidents completely outside our control, which turn our lives and our world upside down. For all groups, the necessity of admission to a Psychiatric Unit depends on their inner ability to stay in a world of reality while dealing with the circumstances they are faced with.

Sadly, the groups of those who live in the fragile world often look and actively seek out those they believe will protect them from harm. The bikie groups, and anti-government groups, the militant groups that get together because they realise there is strength in numbers. They frequently self-medicate. The choice of medication is usually alcohol or illicit drugs. And since both give them some respite, they continue to use until there comes a time when they are in danger of becoming addicted. Then the precariousness of their mental health deteriorates. Sometimes, they become patients when caring families rescue them, and other times, they may become homeless or unwanted on the streets.

Depression is a cruel, overwhelming disease. Time and space to recover, to adjust, to be able to pick up the pieces and return to the world is often needed. Concentrating on oneself is allowed and a period of time in hospital is sometimes necessary.

The underlying idea is that from the moment the patient comes into the hospital, all efforts are made to assist them in returning to the world. The period of time they use the services of the specially trained staff will vary, but the desired outcome is always the same.

Psychiatric Units are not dour places. They are where normalcy is displayed, where mentoring happens, where routines are planned, where treatment is given, and where safety is paramount for everyone.

It is said that, for a little while, the patient leans on the staff and the routines, until, slowly and at their pace, they no longer need to lean. And in a perfect world, this is accomplished.

But no hospital is perfect, and no staff member is either. So sometimes the results take longer than expected, and sometimes the results are very imperfect. Society has to accept that. Just as the real world has prisons for those who cannot live well in society, so do psychiatric hospitals have patients who will never live well in society.

So, there is the need for the capable to see imperfections and follow that with the thought, "There but for the grace of God go I," and then to pause and accept what they do not understand.

The most enterprising young man, who attended the Hospital Emergency Department and was admitted, was the guy who said the Sydney Mafia were chasing him. They were definitely going to kill him. He could spout underworld names like a dictionary. His agitation was out of control. He was medicated and given food and rest. For two days, he repeated his story, and his delusions just escalated with each day. He hid, he tried to remain out of sight, and he would not be calmed.

Day three arrived, and with it, his brother, who was allowed to visit him. Every word he had spoken was true. He was being chased by the Mafia; he was in danger of losing his life for owing money to the Mafia. He had been exceedingly clever in thinking that a hospital might give him cover until his brother blew it.

Now, reader, what would you have done under those circumstances?

You see there is a world that most people don't enter into, unless normalcy becomes too difficult. It is behind the doors of a Psychiatric Unit where staff attend to those whose internal resources are insufficient, or whose external resources are unavailable.

It goes undercover most of the time until someone's mental health deteriorates – perhaps a crime is committed and then its insufficiency is exposed. For a while it is front page news. For a while the doors of a Psychiatric Unit are open, but only to be shut again quickly. It really isn't good news, and the Public does not want to know about its existence.

But you know it is there, quietly taking care of those whose lives have become unstable. It is what we do as a society to protect ourselves, to educate, and to say, "Take heed, protect your mental health." It is precious to you, and you will never know how much until you lose it.

☙

Tiny Tales

Holiday
Like a bird
It descends
Slowly
Wheels touch down
Home.

New Dad 1.
On Plane
Child hoisted
Desperate effort
Quiet reigns.

New Dad 2.
On plane
Child hoisted
Imitating others
Child screams.

ଔ

Boarding School Life in New Zealand

(In the 1950s)

A sense of adventure turned into a peculiar sense of forlornness. Left. Left to stand on my own two feet. *Well, I can do that,* I thought, looking at the forbidding building I was soon to call home.

When you have just emerged from your country town school where life had been a mixture of land, animals, brothers, and loving parents – the city, with its numerous buildings and people everywhere, was a sharp contrast. So too the school. Country schools are nothing like the big, girls everywhere, secondary schools. The only thing the same was the Nuns. Black robed, wimpled head dress with the same rules. Don't run, walk. Be on time. Do as you are told. Look I don't know how they thought a teenager who was used to fields and orchards, and trees to climb, was ever going to heed the restrictions placed on her.

But on that first day, unpacking a small suitcase containing just the bare essentials, this was the scary start of a new life. Then making up a bed allocated to me in the small dormitory of the Boarding school where I was to sleep with a bunch of girls who I didn't know – that was all I could manage to assimilate. The rebellion against restrictions would come later.

Then my parents left to travel back to home, and the boys and the land. We were not farmers, but we had horses, and house cows, and pet lambs, chickens, a dog and a cat, and orchards full of all kinds of fruit trees. How did I learn that silkworms lived on Mulberry trees? Because my brothers grew them on our mulberry tree. How did I learn to ride horses bareback? Simply by swinging my leg over the horse that came up close to the fence I sat on. It wasn't that I was brave; it was simply that the horse was there. I copied everything else that my brothers did. I fell in the stream, climbed the trees, acted as runner for the ball in cricket, (they never let me bat,) had my wits scared out of me by the eels they chased me with, rode my bike off into the sunset with a girlfriend, and in general enjoyed the life of a scallywag. But you do this because your role models are boys. So I didn't like dresses either. Now all of this prepares you for what?

For living carefree, for attempting things most girls don't, for having a go and expecting everything will turn out well. Along the way I did well at school. And the one girl who kept beating me drove me to work harder in my last year of primary school. I simply wanted to do better than her. Well, I did beat her, and that meant I became Dux of the Primary school, and THAT meant I was sent to Boarding school – not as a punishment but to learn more and to learn to be a girl as well. *Huh. Much chance of that happening.*

So you see the eyes that viewed the little bed and the small dresser were not the worldly eyes of the city kids. When girls got into a huddle and left someone out, I thought that was mean, and I wasn't okay with their actions. It simply wasn't my world. And in their turn, I'm not sure they understood me either. I was put into an "A" stream class, but, had they rated me on experience with other girls, I would have rated a Z. I got smarter as the months progressed. I learnt how to follow the rules which had repercussions if I didn't, and to disregard those which I thought didn't matter. At the end of each school day, I spent endless hours talking with my Day scholar "Best Friend". No one seemed to be bothered by that, but the Boarder who spent hours talking to a boy after school, you guessed it, she got expelled. I complied with the 'never to be caught in another girl's cubicle' rule, but I had no idea why this was considered a mortal sin. There were other rules, like never going into the bathroom while another girl was using it, another mortal sin type rule, so yes, I obeyed those rules without question, even if they seemed daft to me.

My first year was spent trying to find my place in this foreign world. I did what the others did, that seemed the safest bet. I learned the routine. Up at the crack of dawn, often to Mass down the road, then breakfast before the school day started. Breakfast was not the bacon and eggs variety; no, it was good and wholesome, stick- to –your- ribs type porridge. I don't think I have eaten it since Boarding School.

Lunches were equally as wholesome and dinner at night was not what anyone could call memorable. And you ate what was given to you. No seconds and no refusals were tolerated. This was often fine by me. Those who didn't like Macaroni cheese pushed it around their plates while I ate theirs and mine. So we all managed; food was shared; what I didn't like, someone else was sure to enjoy a second plateful of – we just swapped plates. I do not remember ever feeling like I was starved. Rather I was adequately complete. And besides, I liked stews and the all-in-together type meals.

Nothing was ever wasted. If not eaten at one meal, it returned under a different guise at the next meal. So we had some very unusual meals sometimes, but who would complain? And even if you did, who would listen? I have to tell you – NO ONE. Not a bad way to run a Boarding school: it was the principle of suck it up and get on with your life. No, wait! There was one person who would listen: God. Now He was spoken to very often. Before Meals, before Bed, and many a time in between. But most of our prayers were not centred on us. Rather, they were centred on those less fortunate than we were, and we were reminded so often of the poor and starving in some mysterious country somewhere on the World Map. There was always someone who was worse off than I, so complaining was a useless waste of time.

My lovely Best Friend was the recipient of all that was good and bad about Boarding School. I think she was often amazed at what went on behind the scenes, but with all the good grace of a best friend, she listened, and said little.

I could have written to Home and maybe complained but all letters were vetted before they were sent, and all letters received were vetted. That was to stop what? Again, I was never quite sure what evil might lurk in a letter.

Home was a distance away, so my parents did not visit. I went home a couple of times a year; the rest of the time I spent at the School. That was life. You embraced it or you drowned. Now if I could sling my leg over a horse, and ride it holding the mane, I could absorb the world I was living in. So I did.

What I struggled with was the girl groups. It's called 'belonging,' and everyone wants to belong. My world was living on the outskirts of these groups because so many of the groups had been formed before I came to the school. They had come up from Primary together, so they stayed together. As an A-grade student, that gave me some status, but the warmth of intimate groups was never there.

Then I moved into my second year, and this time I knew what to expect, and I knew how to help the younger students. But when I got sassy and tried to make the girls stand on their own two feet and buck some of the other rules, the nuns got clever. They put me in charge of the dormitory, which we all called the Baby Dormitory. In reality, they were primary school students in their last years of Primary school. I couldn't really influence them for bad; all I could do was listen to the desperate sobs after lights out and feel the grief of the younger ones. *How could the parents do this to them,* I wondered? *Leaving them a million miles from home!* So, I tried to make them understand they could be like me. See, a fish out of water, but still swimming.

What got me the most was the lack of information about how girls grew! There were lessons on etiquette, but never on health. Never on what to expect as you entered puberty. No lessons, no drawings, no books, no information. The older girls tried to be Mum and give the younger ones knowledge, but what did we know. Zero, Zilch, nothing. So garbled rubbish was passed on from the older groups to the younger groups.

If I ever had anything to really complain about in a girl's Boarding School, it was this: teach them all about puberty. How gross was it that we ended up leaving school with the biggest mishmash of where we came from and how we got into this world. I cannot remember the word 'sex' ever being spoken.

I then did what middle school students do: I rebelled. I led a few of the rebellious and we sneaked into the kitchen after lights out, found cookies and snacked up big time. Collectively, we all got a bollocking after the staff saw the empty tins. But, no one told on the other. My, but it was great a feast for all.

But the second rebellion I led nearly got me excommunicated. Not expelled, you will see, but the Lord would smite me with His mighty hand, and I would never survive it. Well, the bollocking seemed to intimate that. I simply told everyone to stay in bed on a weekday morning. Don't get up, don't go to Mass; we don't have to; it's only Sister Mathews making us get up so early on a cold winter morning. So we stayed in bed, a whole dormitory.

The sound of the voice of the Boarding House Nun in Charge would have raised the roof of the Cathedral. However, I figured God understood. He and I were mates by that time. But I wasn't going to get up on another cold winter morning for one more Nun just so she could get the tick of approval.

Hellfire and damnation followed, but so too did the sleep-ins; we got a lot more of them.

On the kinder side of life in a Boarding House were the steaming hot cups of soup waiting for us after a winter's day at school. We wrapped our hands around these cups that held our "leftover" soup. Everything but the kitchen sink had gone into this cupful, but it was hot, and there was lots of it.

And then there were the evenings after homework was completed. We were sometimes read to on all aspects of etiquette, we were sometimes allowed to dance to music, and how we loved one of the Nuns who really could do ballroom dancing. She took the male role and swirled us left and right, her rosary beads and waist cord flying in the air. We could play board games, and our family of all shapes and sized girls were generous and companionable.

And because we were to stay healthy, we played sport or we walked. Those terrible snake-like formations of girls, marching two by two, up and down the streets of the city, dressed in our suits, Lyle stockings, hats and gloves. And every car that drove past us slowed down to look at the gross sight. We held our heads high, and pretended we couldn't see the spectacle we made as we walked on.

I mentioned Lyle stockings. Those disgusting things may have kept our legs warm but they looked like something out of the last century. And they were held up by those equally disgusting suspender belts. And these stockings, somehow, went into holes, week in and week out, but not for long. Everyone learnt to mend stockings. That was an evening's entertainment in itself getting out the small mushrooms and mending each and every hole. Every pair of stockings would last for years, even if it was more darned than stocking.

Now, one of the advantages about being an A-student was that we were taught French. But only at the most basic of levels.

So it was decided I should attend a French Club in the city. How the teachers found this I do not know. So off I went. My task: to speak French with others learning the language. Except I never got there. Instead, I took the "shopping" orders of other boarders, did their shopping for them and, as a treat, stopped at an Ice Cream Parlour where the owner hid me down in the back of the shop and filled me with cream sundaes. I loved every mouthful. You can't keep a rebellious teenager down, can you? And I still cannot speak French.

Boarding school taught me many things. Like how to keep your shoes shining, your hat in shape, your gloves mended, and we could be relied on to put on a show at a moment's notice. We could recite poetry, some could sing, and we did create some entertaining evenings for ourselves, or for any dignitary who visited. We could dust and clean, and spit and polish, make great beds, and we could study.

Were we well-rounded? Well, who could decide that? Were we full of values and beliefs? You bet we were. Did these values, morals, and beliefs match the "outside" world? A little. Were we prepared for the world we were about to enter into? Not at all.

Years afterwards, and on reflection, I came to understand that those nuns gave their best. It was just that they had no experience to offer that might allow a girl to think she could do anything, or be anything. I started with an *I can do anything* premise, and then found that quashed. Later in my life, I regained that thinking and it became my mantra, and I discovered I actually could do almost anything. I just had to have the motivation to do it.

For each of us going through that time, society itself was developing, and women were emerging. Some went ahead and paved the path for others, and some remained in the confined roles that the school reinforced.

But now?

It seems to me the current Boarding schools have come into this century, and teachers along with them, so the future Marie Curies of this world can step out and into the spotlight and we are the better for them.

The Me Too movement has happened, women's education has become broader, doors have opened, and intelligence ceases to be gender-orientated. There is still the need for Boarding Schools throughout Australia, but we have become more creative in Boarding School parenting and more generous in taking the young and spirited and allowing them space for their development. With this, we shall see a society that is welcoming of change.

☙

The black raven
Croaked and swooped
Cleaning up
Werio's seed

☙

Boss

This is a gruesome story. Let me forewarn you.

As a child I grew up on ten acres of land in a small town in New Zealand. There were orchards on either side of the house, and fruit trees abounded. There were horses, a pet sheep, a pet cow, a cat, lots of chickens, and a dog. And this story is about the dog.

He wasn't called Boss for nothing. He believed himself to be The Boss, thinking he was human, or at least an extension of the human race. He didn't really belong to any one member of the family, he belonged to all. And what possessed my mother to get a bulldog I shall never know. They are notorious for being in charge of all they survey and territorial to the Nth degree.

Perhaps my mother bought him for his protective abilities, which he displayed until told to 'can it' when visitors arrived. Not that he scared them; he just set off his own alarm system until he was ordered to stand down. He knew better than to scare humans, he sort of understood that they might be just a little further up the pecking order than he was. But as an alarm, he was superb. Unless it was us, as children, coming home from school, and then the alarm didn't go off. No, he just slobbered all over us, showing deep dog love and appreciation that we had returned to the kennel.

However, there was a side to this dog that no words and no actions could deter. No other animals were allowed on his property unless they were *his* animals. Cats take note. Don't venture up one of his trees. Dogs had to be introduced to him, and once he had given them his careful scrutiny they would be tolerated.

How did he make this distinction? It was always a wonder to me that he could accept the horses and even run around with them in the paddock until they literally kicked over the traces, and he scampered off. I think he had some idea of a pack. His pack was humans and his animals. The family cat never took a blind bit of notice of him; she just turned her nose up at him if he was in a frisky moment. Cats do distain so well.

He was a house and garden dog. Lived inside and slept outside and could demolish any amount of food scraps that fell from the table, albeit dropped very surreptitiously to him. What gave him away was the dribble he could manufacture at the sight of food. Disgusting.

But woe betides any other animal setting foot on his property. The first cat to do so didn't live to tell the tale. And we had to keep quiet about it because it probably belonged to some neighbour, somewhere. It was buried with due ceremony right away in the far corner of the paddock.

The first dog to trespass on his property he attempted to drown in the stream that flowed through our property. My brother rescued it in the nick of time. We wondered how many others he had disposed of this way. And then we also wondered how he learned to do this. Wasn't that amazing?

So I think the local animals passed on the word about him until the fateful adventure of the 'possum, one of those long-tailed furry creatures introduced into New Zealand by the Australian exporters.

It came into the apple orchard. Now, Boss could not climb trees. He did try, and he could get up onto the lower branches, but he mainly stood at the bottom of the tree and looked up into it with an unwavering stare. You knew something was up there. He watched and waited.

Night after night the possum eluded him. He knew it was there and he stood to attention beneath whichever tree it was up. Did he get frustrated? Never. He maintained his vigil and his determination to get the intruder the minute it made a mistake.

Well, the mistake didn't happen at the tree's site; it happened inside the house.

One night, the possum made the mistake of scampering over the roof, taking a shortcut between the orchards. It would have survived except for the fact that it went over an unused chimney and fell down to the bottom, right into my bedroom. Soot and the possum made an unwelcome landing on my toys sitting in the disused fireplace. I yelled, and the Boss came running. He knew his protective role in the family, and then his nose caught the smell.

The door was open and Boss bounded in, and it was on for young and old. The possum went under the bed, and so did the dog. It ran down the passageway and into the lounge, and so did the dog. It went into the kitchen, the boy's room, every room in the house it went, Boss hot on its tail. I don't know how many times it went around the house, a very big, rambling old farm-style house. The family kept ducking for cover, but the dog was on a mission.

Then, the two of them ended up in the bathroom, and World War Three erupted. At the finish, there was only one creature alive. The other one was covered in blood and my distressed mother ran a bath for Boss and put him in it. My father did what fathers are supposed to do and dug another plot down at the end of the paddock.

My mother tenderly washed the dog looking for cuts, scratches, and signs of wounds and Boss happily let her do this. Until my mother looked up and said she couldn't see a mark on him, he was just enjoying the warm bath and the attention he was receiving. The wily old bulldog thought this was his just due.

After all he had saved his family from the intruder.

The family lived off that story for years, and my dad learned to put netting over unused chimneys.

Boss grew older, like the rest of us, still in the role of protector, until he could no longer defend his family, and he quietly slipped away into Doggie Heaven.

My belief is that we are all going to be reunited; the heavens of cats and dogs, and pets of all descriptions will one day enjoy their people's company again. Think of the stories that will be appreciated and retold with great fervor, gusto, and embellishment. Think of the fun we'll have together.

Did you know we had a cow who thought she was human too; she milked every day of the year just to keep us nourished. Unheard of for cows. Her raspy lick of love nearly took three layers of skin off your arm when she cuddled up. Will there be room for her in the pet heaven? I wonder.

ℭ

Tiny Tales

Animal stories:

1.
Little feet patter
Dog smiles
Shifts in basket
Makes room.

2.
Large kennel
Boy talks
Dog listens
Warm Brown eyes
understanding.

3.
Cat relaxes
Sun burns
Ears trimmed
Cancer: White cats fate.

4.
Thoroughbred dog
Lies in silence
Puppies arrival
How'd that happen?

5.
Cat castrated,
Home from vet,
Runs amok
Throughout the house.

6.
Slightly open window
Kittens pushed inside
All saved. Clever Tabby.

7.
Leg swings over,
Horse whinnies
Bareback ride
Around the paddock.

8.
Leg swings over,
Horse whinnies,
Ducks head,
Kid into mud.

9.
Baby foal
wanting fun
Chases child
Safety in
gooseberry bush.

10.
Cow complaining
Kicks bucket
Father wild, kicks cow
Broken toe.

⊗

Catch Phrase

Shouts of laughter
Crazy Game
No one forgets it
Fun.

Gold Coast memories
Pent-house
Two pairs of sisters
Fun

ଔ

Discussions with a Taxi Driver

She came out of her night class at 8 p.m., and the weather had changed for the worse. The light drizzle she had encountered after work had become heavy rain, the kind where the droplets pounded down and your hand in front of your face became difficult to see.

She could catch the bus, as she usually did on a Tuesday evening, but that meant a considerable walk down to the bus stop and getting wetter by the second. Perhaps tonight she would take a taxi home, and the thought of home and a warm bath and a late supper seemed like a comforting end to a long day.

She scanned the street while sheltering under the eaves of the gentle old building that housed the university's evening classes, classes designed to get that precious certificate that would enable her to begin to practice as a Nanny. With that in her hand she was going to travel, to see the world, and it couldn't come soon enough.

"Taxi," she called as a car came in sight, its red light on on top of the roof barely visible through the rain. She waved in its direction and was relieved to see the car come towards her. A quick sprint to the back door, and she was in.

"Thanks," she said as she gave him her address.

He gave her a smile, and commented on the unseasonable weather.

"You another one doing night classes?" he asked. "I pick up a lot around this time from the Uni."

"Yes," she replied, her fair hair falling out from the jacket she had pulled up while running towards the taxi.

Over the next few kilometres, he engaged her in conversation about what she was studying and what she planned on doing with her Childcare certificate. In return, she learned he was new to the country and driving because he was waiting for his application for residency.

After a few minutes, she snuggled down into the seat, tired from her working day. But he continued talking. Did she live at home? No. Did she live with others? No. Where did she work? And with this last question she started to feel a little uncomfortable. She looked out the window, and wondered why he was taking the Kent Street route. That surely was the long way, but she shrugged – he was new to the city.

The houses flew by. How did she get to work each day? By bus. Which bus did she take? How long did it take for her to get to work? She tried to avoid answering, and when she did answer she kept her answers brief.

The rain was unrelenting, and home was beginning to be a very desirable place. She let her mind slip away as he continued talking, and the conversation just wafted over her until she noticed they were taking the route through the park, definitely a way she would not have taken.

And then she heard it—the click as the car doors all went into lock mode. She knew about this because her mother had a car that could be locked, like this, which is supposed to prevent children from opening a door.

BODY FOUND IN CENTENNIAL PARK read the headlines, above the picture of a young, blonde girl lying amongst the sodden wet leaves of a very old, gnarled Fig tree.

CR

Forgiveness

Paul looked forlornly at the letter he took from his pocket. He had really only meant to be helpful. Just a little hop, skip and jump down to the letterbox, and yes, there was a letter. Then Timothy from next door called out and invited him to come and play, and he did. He ended up forgetting about the letter as the football was kicked high and low between them. And then the Button brothers came and joined in the game, and so they played outside in the park for a couple of hours, chasing footballs and tackling, and making up rules and just having a ten-year-olds happy afternoon.

How was he going to explain to his mother that THE letter had arrived? – the one she had been down to the letterbox for every day now for two weeks, hoping to get. She had said to them all to let her get the mail because there was something very special coming in the mail and she wanted to be the first to open it. And he really hadn't meant to be disobedient, but he thought perhaps, with his luck, he could make it arrive. And it had, and then he just got distracted and went on to play with his street friends.

What should he do? If he took it in now, his mother would know that it had been in his pocket all afternoon. She would know he had disobeyed her. He had watched her come back from the letterbox each day looking so sad he had thought to himself that if he went it was sure to be there. After all, he was the one that found all the lucky four-leaf clovers, the pen that Patrick lost, and even his father's car keys, which he swore blind he had put on the kitchen table. Well, Paul had found them down the back of the sofa, but he didn't like to contradict his father.

What would his father say? This was not going to end up being a happy day, was it? So he thought long and hard. The letter was getting sticky with grass and football-stained hands, so he couldn't put it back in the letter box. His mother would know; she always knew these things.

So he trudged back up to the house, scuffing his shoes as he walked, tears starting to form in his eyes. Through the back door into the kitchen, he went, and silently held the letter out to his mother as she stirred a pot over the stove. And he stood and looked at her as she took the letter and with trembling hands opened it.

Tears rained down her face and an unbelievable smile broke through the waterfall as she tried to speak. "Oh, Paul," she said, "thank you, thank you." And for some inexplicable reason, she hugged him. It was going to be alright after all. She was going to forgive him. "Oh, Paul," she said, "this is the best news, the very best news, and I am going to share it with you. Your father and I asked if we could adopt another child, someone we could all love and care for. We so wanted another little boy, one just like you. And now we will be able to. This letter says that there is a little boy who desperately wants a new home, and a big brother too, one like you. Oh, Paul," she said, "just wait until your father gets home."

⊂⊃

I Started Life in a Blanket, in a Church ...

I sometimes think my life story could be compared to fiction. If it was made into a book, who would believe it?

Well, you just wouldn't.

Let me start at the beginning; even my beginnings are really unbelievable. I don't know who my mother was, and because of that, I do not know who my father was either. My mother left me wrapped in a warm blanket, and because she at least must have felt something for me, she put me into a Church—a large but modern church right up near the altar. The Church was in Queensland, Australia.

The priest who found me did all the right things. He contacted the police and then they gave me over to the Nuns who ran the Orphanage. They were Josephite nuns and, for lack of a more original name, they called me Josephine. I think they thought that the great St Joseph would take me under his wing and what ... teach me carpentry? I stayed at the Orphanage for a year because the current financial depression meant that newborns were not so readily adopted. But at one year of age, I was, so they tell me, a happy smiling child, and the nuns almost fought over me in their eagerness to be my "Mother". I know this because the Priest who met me at the altar became my mentor throughout my school life.

But it fell my lot in life to go to a home with "new" parents. They were not young but I wasn't to know that. Their caring of me was so perfect. How could one little girl get such wonderful parents? My free spirit was allowed to be free. My questions were answered; my little soul was nourished. Schooling seemed easy to me because both my parents spent hours with me, helping me to understand maths, and english, and history, and best of all geography. Through their eyes, I saw the countries of the world. They ignited in me a desire to visit the places they showed me in the huge Atlas that took pride of place on the bookshelf.

We were not wealthy, but I was not to know that either because we grew much of our food and bottled the fruit or preserved the vegetables. Our lives were as perfect as a family's could be, until midway through my secondary schooling. That was when I learned grief. My parents were killed in an accident.

It was no one's fault unless you could blame God for sending a storm and making the roads so slippery that my dad lost control of his pride and joy. He drove a vintage car, you see, which we had all loved.

There were no relatives, only me. I owned a house, and I had no one.

What happened next was a fork in the road of my unbelievable life story. There was a Nun who was about to leave convent life, and Father Steele, my mentor, asked me if she could come to live with me. She would be the adult in charge of me, and in return, she had a home to go to. It seemed like it was a good fit.

The name my companion returned to was Amy.

Amy was about forty and she was the good fit Father thought she might be. She received her dispensation from Rome and ceased to be a Nun. Instead, she returned to University and commenced her studies. Her ambition was to study International Mediation, and only the Bond University had this very elevated study on offer. So, for me, I continued at school, and along with Amy, I listened to and often took part in her studies. She would practice her assignments on me. I grew to be a very good actor and she grew to be a marvellous listener. She had clever thoughts and divergent ideas when I was going down a path of destructiveness as the imaginary Prime Minister of some fictitious country. We stopped potential wars, and started community shelters, prevented child abuse, and business catastrophes. Our companionship grew into a warm and lasting friendship.

In the three years she studied this course, I studied almost every page with her. And I wanted to follow in her footsteps. But hearing this wish, she asked me to pause. She made the wise suggestion that I would be better to follow my first love of geography. She suggested doing this in a practical way by studying Journalism and visiting countries around the world using my writing skills. Then, later, the experience I had gained would be a perfect base for returning to university and, yes, taking the course she had undertaken. She painted such a world for me I thought it encompassed all my heart's desires.

And that was what I did. I studied Journalism, and I worked and accepted assignments that took me to many countries, some at war, some United Nations controlled, some emerging from a third-world status and shifting towards a second-world status. And while I was doing this, she went to America and joined the United Nations. Our lives were so often out of kilter and in various time zones, but we never ceased our communications. And like Father Steele, she never ceased to encourage me or to support me when the situations I encountered dragged me down to almost the dust beneath my feet.

I like to think that she benefitted from my experiences and used them in her peacekeeping role. And I found she was right. The journalistic career I had embarked on created so many experiences of how life was lived in so many countries of the world, it changed me. I learned to be compassionate; I learned that clear-cut right and wrong thinking had to be moderated with practicalities.

So it took me until I was nearly thirty-eight before I returned to Australia and made the decision to study again. This time, I knew exactly what I wanted. I needed the skills to assist in confrontations and the power plays to enable some form of compromise to occur. I wanted to see a better world. I never married because no man could keep up with the wanderlust I had developed. It simply wouldn't have been fair.

But Amy's pathway included marriage. She found a like-minded widower working in the United Nations with whom she shared dreams, and so she married him.

I found the return to study difficult. I itched to travel; I wanted to record the world's emerging sense of determination. So I struggled, but experience had always taught me well, and my experiences and my motivation bolstered my ambition.

I achieved my degree, but that was simply a title. It was the foundation skills that I wanted. When I thought I was ready, I took my journalism and mediation skills and returned to the world stage.

I worked for my own government, and I repaid the goodness and kindness I had grown up with and the intellectual stimulation Amy had developed in me. I went down a new path. I worked in business, big business — business that took me into a range of third-world countries. I stepped between those with the mantle of power and those wanting truth, and there was not an hour or a day that I allowed those wars to crush my spirit. I worked behind the scenes; only those who knew me well knew where I would be on a daily basis. I learnt the foundations of so many religions and the consequences of not upholding the practices of those religions in order to ensure they were incorporated into every field I worked in.

And I crept into little churches on my travels and spoke to the God that gave me my mother, and my parents; the mentor that He blessed me with, and the friend and guide that He gave me when I needed it most.

As I said at the beginning, my life story reads like fiction. But I have learned one thing. Survival means that you take the advantages offered to you, from the blanket my mother wrapped me in to the Nun who left the convent for another calling, and you find how these advantages allow you to contribute. You use everything you have been blessed with and you make a difference, and that difference gives your soul its truest satisfaction.

I am older and wiser now, and mentoring has become my new role in life. I share my experiences, my successes and my failures. I watch the eager faces who will be the future warriors for peace in our world.

And I want to say to them all, "I started my life in a blanket, learn from this."

CR

Tiny Tales

Postie

Dad's gift
Express post
Child's Excitement
Dolls house
Replica of home.

Happiness

Photos
Neat and tidy
Huge smile
Made a memory
Today.

Blind

Husband gagged
Recipe disaster
Salt instead of sugar
Broken spectacles.

I'm a Believer in Miracles. Are You?

I probably wasn't until I met Lisa.

Over the years, what I had learnt about myself was that I could rely on myself to adapt to most circumstances; I knew my strengths. But I didn't allow any weaknesses. I didn't truly see myself with many weaknesses at all. Life threw me many curly questions and I found answers for them. Being an orphan either makes you or breaks you, and in my case, when they gave me my bag and $100 dollars then set my feet firmly outside the front gates of the orphanage at the age of sixteen, I knew I was a man now. I didn't look back.

I had a paper run within a week, and a delivery run within two. I had a room with a roof over my head, and I knew that working in any form of restaurant would make sure I was fed. I delivered meals on a bike that I found left deserted in the park, and after a few months that bike became a moped. I didn't even know the word 'enterprising' in those days because my schooling had been poor, but life had taught me plenty.

I had a goal, and I had a work ethic, and both of these things kept me out of harm's way. I didn't do drugs or alcohol. I saved money. I had few friends because I simply didn't have the time for them.

By the time I was twenty-one, I had rented a small apartment. It wasn't in the best part of town, but neither was it in the worst part of town. There was room for the moped and me.

Did I miss friendships? Yes, I did, but I couldn't ask anyone else to live my structured life, and I would not give up my goal for any other person. I was going to become wealthy, and with that wealth, I was going to live in an apartment where I could look out on the city from a great height and know that I had made it. It had to be an apartment at some height because that was the only way I could actually see that I had climbed out of the smallness of an orphanage and had succeeded.

It took me until I was thirty to get that apartment. By that time, I had a franchise in the world of fast food and employed about thirty people. I had swapped my moped for a certain to-get-you-there car. And no, it wasn't flash, but it was reliable.

And then into my life walked Suzanne. She literally just walked in to negotiate with me over the land between her shop and my franchise. I recognised her immediately; she was a carbon copy of me. She was energetic, enthusiastic, and she had a head for business.

Our business heads became a partnership, which in turn became a relationship. Her clothing range was exquisite. She started with her own designs and her ability to make her own clothes. Together, we bought the land and expanded both businesses.

She came to live with me and we married quietly one long weekend, and I knew happiness that I had thought would never be mine.

Susanne came from a noisy but happy family. She was the eldest of six children, and her parents had worked hard to provide for them all. They were the reason Suzanne had determined she wanted more. They were the reason she had used her ability to create clothing for those who could pay her prices for exclusive designs.

It took us about three years to realise that we had material possessions and each other, and yet there seemed to be something missing. A void might better describe it. We had discussed having children and both felt this was just a natural progression in our relationship. But it didn't happen. I think we were both almost struck dumb by this. We had control over our busy lives, and a relationship that was strong, and with all this, we were unable to have children.

The doctors, and we saw plenty, said there was no apparent reason for being unable to conceive. We were just one of the few couples where nature could not be forced into being creative.

So we decided to wait and work.

And then one terrible day there was an accident on the road outside our businesses. A young mother lost her life because of a careless, inexperienced driver. We rescued her little girl from the back seat of her car and kept her warm and safe while the ambulance people worked on her mother.

It was a futile attempt. We were asked to take the child to her grandparents' home, which we did. There was no father alive, we were told. The grandparents were an elderly couple living in a small but well-kept home, who had now lost a son and a daughter-in-law. And their sadness was so painful.

We stayed in touch.

The child's name was Lisa, and somehow we became a set of foster parents. We developed a great fondness for Lisa's grandparents and Lisa enjoyed living in two homes. It used to be her favourite story, telling everyone she lived in two homes. And, as she grew and developed, it just became a natural evolution that she came to live with us after her grandparents passed away.

We shared our knowledge of business with her and took her to parts of the world she had only read about in books. We showed her how to source materials from countries where it was their resource product, and she learnt from me how to stay on a budget and balance the books.

She, in turn, taught us about how deeply a child can love and how deeply a child can be loved in return.

I told you I believe in miracles, and the day she came into my life Lisa fulfilled my life in a way I would never have thought possible. I did wonder if in some way, it might have been God's way of apologising to Suzanne and I.

Or was He just saying, *I saved this special child for you because you knew what it was like to grow up without parents?*

Mmm. What do you think?

◌౩

I shot a story
Into the email
It fell
Rejected.

◌౩

More Than Meets the Eye

He came into the room, his eyes roving over the group studying the new artworks. His attention was caught by a group looking intently at the painting with a red sticker saying SOLD attached to it. A pricey number, around $10,000. He didn't think it was one of his better works but he would be grateful to the buyer. He moved a little closer and heard them discussing his brush strokes, the perspective he had given the face turned towards the light. The fine skin, the smile, and the eyes so clear, silky brown in colour. He knew what captivated this audience, as it had captivated him too.

Not the beauty of the face, which was really almost plain, but the eyes sparkling with humour and looking knowingly at the painter. From everywhere you positioned yourself; the eyes seemed to follow you.

He had never felt so vulnerable before. He had painted this portrait and the eyes had seemed to see deep within, and he had felt naked, as though she knew.

He wanted to reach out to her, to explain himself, to defend himself, to ask for forgiveness for his careless living. And yet he couldn't. He could only paint what he saw in front of him. And his brush strokes were not perfect, he could not bring himself to steady his hand and to do her justice.

But he could paint the eyes. He could paint the knowingness, the blueness and the depths that held him mesmerised. Yes, he did the eyes justice. They were the one perfect feature in the painting, and they were worth the money offered for his work of art.

And he longed for the friendship those eyes offered, to go beyond the unreachableness they contained. He wanted the wisdom they held and the hope and generosity they told of, that made life worth living every moment.

And yet he knew that this would be forever denied to him, as the soft folds of her dark blue habit fell around her head and shoulders, and the rosary beads remained, held so steadfast in her hands, her small bible on her lap.

◌੪

Visitors

Dog's hair rising
Ears flattening
Stands alert.
Knuckles on door.

Today

Morning.
Alarm at 7 am
Doona 7.30 am
Slippers at 8 am
Day.

◌੪

Multi-tasking

Multi-tasking is a breeze for women. I mean here I am riding a bus into the city; going over thousands of jolting bumps; answering a bus rider who wants to know what perfume I am wearing; thinking of the phone calls I need to make before the end of the day; wondering if I should be doing a book launch at the forthcoming meeting, and as a side venture, I am constructing thoughts for a story.

I know exactly why women are so smart … … it is because they have to be.

Remember the days when one child tugged at your sleeve asking where his sports gear was, while your husband asked for another slice of toast, as you prepared school lunches, and tried to keep your Nurse's uniform crumple-free at least until you got to work. Now that's multi-tasking.

I'm not complaining. Men's virtues include being single minded, focused, and absolute. Now, each of those attributes is worthy, but it doesn't get things done, does it? Well, let me concede, it may get things done, but it's a slow process. Like male cops finding a murderer, it takes months. I think that's why women are being encouraged to join the Police force. They rack up the clues, sort through them quickly and have a guilty party in no time at all.

And give a woman the job of organising a show and you'll be left gasping at the speed with which she accomplishes it.

The only men I can think of who can process really quickly are rappers. Those are the musicians who can talk underwater.

And they just go with a train of thought a bit like a crazy state of mind, their thought processes encompassing fact and fiction. I'm just not sure they are processing reality.

I think it's why women live longer than men because when men retire it's like their single focus in life has gone (work) and trying to find a new focus is difficult. Multi-tasking women, on the other hand, just go from one job to the next, except they have a little more time to execute their skills when retired.

Multi-tasking requires something only women do well, for another reason too. They can leave themselves out of the equation to get the 6, 7, 8 tasks done. But try this with men, or young folk for that matter, whose framework is living enveloped in "me" thinking. Usually, me first, and second, and what was it you wanted third?

It's not that women leave themselves out completely. They just multi-task with five minutes randomly taken for me, and they build their satisfaction that way.

Sitting in the lunch bar, I am watching. Each woman is eating quickly to get on to the next task. Each man is sitting taking time to well, just take time. It's a gender-related thing. Even the people behind the counter: women answering questions, getting food, wrapping food, taking money, while the guys are just making coffee, repetitively, but focused.

I see a mum go by, baby in a papoose cradle, child at foot, shopping to do, children to feed. All of her is working. Arms for the purchases, shoulders for the infant, hands for a child, ops, the call of nature …. Of course, a potty stop in the middle of everything. Been there, darling, and know that your system is running on adrenaline.

Not quite the same when the husband walks through the door about 6 pm and says, "I'm home. Is the coffee on?" looking for his multi-tasking wife. One day you hope for a surprise: "I'm home. How can I help?" or "Shall I bath the children?"

Aaah, wishful thinking.

Can't you laugh at the etiquette books of yesteryear that told you how to keep your husband was to have his slippers ready when he came home, with a quiet ale beside his favourite chair.

But back to multi-tasking, the point I began at, women are so good at this because of their smart, adaptable, creative, intelligent abilities, don't you think? Need any more adjectives?

The world needs us.

❧

Tiny Tales

2-year-old legs
4 furry legs
Full speed ahead
Happiness

Sharp turn
Attention Lapsed
Scrunch post
Air blue
Car dinged

Grumpy Mare
In paddock
Little Boy swinging her tail
Silence.

Zoom time
Family faces
All talking at once
COVID Bliss

&

Once a Spy Always a Spy

His eyes were old but his mind was clear. It often amazed him that, because the signs of older age were evident, people assumed that his faculties had diminished. But he guessed that the young these days who had little experience with older people just made these assumptions. He played along with them, too, and he had to admit to himself he got many a laugh out of waiting until they least expected it, and then joined in the conversation with some brilliant comment, usually backed by political or scientific facts, and waited for their reaction.

It was one of these nights when he sat with his pint in the quaint Pub in Tessletown that he became the owner of information that truly distressed him.

He had started by sitting at a table drinking and listening to the pub music when a group of young men came and sat at the next table. They gave him a glance or two then dismissed him as old and unable.

Well, he was old, and it was true he couldn't run. He shambled rather than walked, but that was just his arthritis playing up. His grey hair was sparse but neat, and yes, he hadn't bothered dressing up for the occasion. He'd caught the bus, comfortable in his tweed jacket and rather well-worn trousers. He enjoyed a drink or two in the out-of-the-way pubs. The publicans were friendly, the food was good. And there was no one waiting for him at home. His daughter wasn't due to visit until the following Sunday. He usually found another single person and spent a sociable hour or so before catching the last bus home.

This routine gave him a great deal of pleasure. New faces, new people to listen to his stories, and new information to share with his daughter each week.

But tonight was different. The logs in the fireplace burned warmly. His drink was going well with the plate of Irish stew he had before him, but the conversation that he heard from the table near him chilled his soul. He continued his dinner, and his act of being old and unseen, as his sharp mind recorded what he heard. He quietly took stock of the four men around the table. Their ages, their clothing, their angry demeanour. The whiskey that followed the beer sometimes lifted their voices.

Then one of the men stood up and curtly told the other three that the next meeting would be at his home – tomorrow at 6 pm sharp – and they all pulled on their winter jackets and left the pub.

And his dilemma began. This was information about a terrorist cell. Everyone in Britain had been asked to stay on alert for information, after the aftermath of the killings on London Bridge. Well, he had plenty of information. But he also knew he was the only patron anywhere near them who could have heard them. And this meant he would have placed himself in danger. An old fellow like him would be found in a ditch somewhere and few townspeople would care. Except maybe his card-playing mates.

Did he want to be a hero? Not really.

So his engineering brain tumbled with ideas. The four men had spoken in Arabic, thinking he would not understand their talk. How could he have told them of the years he spent studying their language, that his earlier years he had spent working in undercover positions providing information for the government intelligence agency Mi5. His retirement had come after his wife had died and he had shifted to where his daughter taught at

College, just to keep a watchful eye on her. Although slowly it had become her keeping a watchful eye on him. But, their mutual respect and deep love for each other was the foundation for an open and generous relationship between them.

He debated sharing what he knew with her and wondered aloud if that would also put her in danger. He debated sharing his knowledge with his long-time friend and ex-Commissioner for Mi5, but that brought the information back to the pub and his proximity to them.

And then he had a masterful idea. He would publish the information he had overheard. There were four different newspapers in the city. He would buy space in all four papers. Each newspaper would contain some of the information he had gleaned. Put together it would create a picture Mi5 would act on. He would buy the advertisements under a variety of names; there would be no trace back to him. But he would frequent a few different pubs while the intelligence network did its job.

He knew how to cover his tracks; that was the easiest part. Writing up the overheard plans in a way that was believable was the next step.

But for a man with his vast experience, he considered this a fitting swansong to a career as a spy. No one survived in this field without above-average intelligence, and although age may have crept up on him, it had not diminished his ability to be creative.

A small part of him wanted the four to understand that they had been taken down by an elderly man, well past his prime in looks and physique, just to see the looks on their faces. But he would have to be content with the inner warmth of the knowledge that, once a spy, always a spy.

◌

Nature, Red in Tooth and Claw

Autumn, the season for the burnished leaves, the rust-coloured leaves, those shaped like curls, brittle like old bones, red in tooth and claw. The myriads of leaves that swirled with the wind, all shapes and sizes, finding gutters, roofs, ground and garden as they covered them in carpets that only nature could provide.

And there, in the midst of the carpet, a face peered out, full of smiles, twinkling eyes, and curly hair. She threw the leaves into the air and watched them land. She threw them again, and the wind caught them and tossed them around her before allowing them to settle again. And she laughed. Then she giggled, and her little feet, enclosed in small gumboots, ran through the leaves until she lost her footing and, with an unceremonious thump, landed on the large pile of leaves recently raked up by her father.

"Daddy, watch me … watch me," she gasped, as she pulled herself up. "I'm flying like the leaves."

And her father turned to see the face creased with a smile so wide and open that he rested his rake to see her run into the pile again and once again take an unceremonious trip into the leaves.

And he thought to himself that the joy those autumn leaves were giving her was so much more important than his raking them up to take them to the bonfire. And he wondered again, as he had wondered so many times before if he had been visited by an angel.

How had she come into his life, this full of energy, little two-legged dynamo? How had he been so lucky to have this perfect child. So guileless, so enchanting and so loving

He knew that his wife had made this child to be the delight she could not provide, as her disease had slowly taken her from him. And, as he glanced skyward, he mouthed a thank you to her for leaving him with someone so beautiful, as a reminder of her, and he promised to take good care of her.

And the leaves swirled in reply and settled like a cape around his daughter, protecting her.

ᘏ

Night time
Bed warm
Husband snores
Moon shines
Drifting off

ᘏ

Please Tell Me What Dying Means?

"Please tell me what dying means?"

"Please tell me why she had to die"

"Please tell me why she has left me."

"Where has she gone to?"

"Please tell me did she love me?"

"Why am I hurting?"

"Why did she leave me? What did I do?"

"What can I do with my sadness? What can I do to get better? When will I see her again?"

"Please, please, help me I don't understand. Can I go and be with her? Please let me."

These were some of the words that came out of his mouth. He came to see me twice a week, and if his mother had seen his broken heart as he came through the door, she would never have taken her own life. He was nine years old.

I know some people see suicide as the ultimate in selfish acts. In very few cases, that is not correct.

I have talked with and been with those who see no other way to escape the depression and pain they are in. Some whose world has become so small, so tiny, that they no longer see anyone other than themselves. And in themselves, they cannot trust.

Because their world is so diminished and they wish to leave it does not make their act selfish. It does make their world intolerable, and my job is to make them see their inner resources, and their external resources.

But, when there is no one in their lives to strengthen them and they carry through with the act, what then?

The fallout is terrible for all who have connections with the person who has died. But especially for those so young they cannot make sense out of the actions of someone near and dear to them.

A nine-year-old boy confronting the loss of a parent, when the act is deliberate, lives in the agony of what is forever and the agony of 'did he cause the parent to die'.

So, to answer the first question of what dying means is a slow, step-by-step answer, with each step clear and in language that can be understood. Even when the action means forever, and that concept is not developed yet in a child, it can be likened to losing a favourite toy or a pet. It can and must be likened to something that the child can relate to.

When a parent suicides the counselling hour is an hour of time that is spent answering the almost unanswerable questions. It is an hour of heartbreak, and the counsellor is not immune.

If there is any religion in the child's life Heaven can be presented. But if there isn't then the explanations must be in accord with what the other parent agrees with. But something has to make sense to that child for this immediate period of time. And no answer is the same. It isn't a glib "this is the way the book sees it". But it is often helped by travelling on the same path as the child. They have an imagination that wants to fill the gaps, and they have a need-to-know answer to their level of understanding.

Each step on the pathway they are on helps to create an understanding of death as being forever, in this life. They can describe, imagine, and draw death and, with you beside them, they will integrate this knowledge. Your role it to support each stage and each step and to spend time as the concepts are explored.

But it is a whole new world to answer why she had to die. And the child expects an answer because you are the adult. And you they rely on. And it can be satisfactory for a child to hear that you do not know why she had to die either. And that this answer may come along someday when both of you are older.

The reassurance of why she has left the child is direct and straightforward. She didn't leave you. She left behind all the things that caused her pain. And you were not one of those things; you never ever were one of the things she wanted to leave behind.

Where has she gone to? Heaven if that concept is understood. Into another world outside our world, if that concept is understood. The night sky provides a vastness that helps this understanding. But she can never come back from that new world. Think about this – you will be introducing the concept of forever to them. And that is one concept that has to be reinforced often because they will expect her to reappear.

Why do I hurt? Because you loved her. And to lose what you have loved so much causes a pain in all sorts of places in our bodies. Where do you feel this hurt? Although little ones will refer to it being in their heart. What can be offered to relieve the physical hurt?

What did I do? Nothing. She loved you, but she hurt so much she wanted to leave this human life. How often they blame themselves. And every time they visit you, you start with the fact that they were loved, and that they were not the reason their mother left.

It follows that the child cannot go to be with her. Perhaps when they are an old man, they can do this. But not now. And you stay with the now. You stay in the world of the child to see when they need comforting, when they need explanations, when they need silence, when they need distraction.

There are some explanations of how the brain works, and how sometimes the brain does not work properly. This can be shown with drawings and pictures. Pictures are solid objects and rational explanations can be given. But it must always be accompanied by the reassurance that their brain has none of these deficiencies and that neither does the remaining parent have these deficiencies.

One of the questions that is not asked but thought about is the overwhelming question: If Mum can do this, will Dad do it too? This is followed by the almost unimaginable horror because then I am bereft. How will I live?

Opening this discussion is easy because it is straightforward. "Do you ever worry…? is how the question is framed. And the small face shows relief that someone "gets it."

In young children, there is innocence and openness. The questions will usually be answered and the thinking will become transparent.

With the child's permission, the other parent may become involved. Suggestions may be made that enable the parent to treat the child's loss with love. Even in the midst of their loss, the two can help each other.

Children will not dwell on their loss because they can be distracted by day-to-day life, but when they need that individual attention and the questions are direct, it is time to stop, listen, and answer.

The child who said he could see his father every night was thought to be fantasising, until he told his mother exactly how his father had died – a fact kept from the child. She was horrified but he was completely accurate, and he explained his father stood at the end of his bed and talked with him intermittently. He was not frightened of his father, and his father stayed for just a few minutes each time until one day, he never returned. In those talks his father had reassured him of his love and was apologetic about leaving him. And the child supported the mother as they both grieved.

How long does a child grieve? It is an unanswerable question. As long as it takes for that small person to grieve. There will be many times when the grief is fresh because of something that happens in his or her life. But each episode will be less than the one before.

And what supports a child is the simplest of actions: love and time. Resources are made available: grandparents and teachers. Without intruding but with presence, at the child's pace at the child's enquiry as the child needs.

A child with a pet, like a dog, may use that animal to share thoughts with. To speak naturally, hold and be comforted by the therapeutic dog or cat. Animals know language is often not needed and they have an innate sense of giving body comfort with the wisdom to just be with the child.

The healing comes about as transparency is shown, and openness about the loss is normal for the child. It comes as those left behind model resilience in living a different life, without forgetting the important person who is gone.

And in the years that follow you will hear your words of comfort repeated as these children know exactly what their friends need in a time of grief, and you will have given them tools that they have been able to share.

And your job is done.

೦೩

Reminiscing

She sits in her new and very modern chair, the one her children have given her. Now, when had they given it to her? She remembers it was a birthday but was it last year, or the year before? She can't quite remember which.

But she knows it is 2023 because the large calendar in her room tells her that. It is electric so she never has to rewind, or reset it. And that's a blessing. She also knows how to push the required buttons in this chair to enable her legs to lift; it's so much more comfortable with her legs up. Although she has pressed the wrong button from time to time, and lowered her back support instead of lifting her legs. But she doesn't tell her children or grandchildren that when they come to visit.

She likes to appear bright and bubbly when they visit, even though it is a strain sometimes. She tells herself listening to their chatter is just so interesting. The things they can do, the modern world they live in. It stretches her mind to hear them talk about the new robot they bought, one for doing the laundry. Imagine that, it is programmed to sort the laundry, program the washing machine and then wait for the wash to finish so it can do a dry cycle. Laundry, the bane of her life. With three children, she had shirts, sports clothes, school uniforms, and play clothes in abundance, times four of everything. She included her husband in that figure as he changed his clothing every day, come rain or come shine.

What an appropriate expression, she thought. *Come rain or come shine*, whether you used the outside line when it was fine or the inside line when it was wet. Her husband had strung up that line in the laundry all those years ago. How she had needed it then, with nappies and clothes occupying the line at least five days a week.

And she thought with deep affection of the man who had stood by her side for seventy of her ninety-four years. He had never learned to be a carpenter, he had never studied trades, no, he had been destined for the professions, an accountant, and a good one at that. But since they were extremely poor, he learned to turn his hand to everything, just as she had done.

They had come from two very different families, not wealthy but hard working. How lucky they had been that both families had a respect for education. He was educated to become an accountant; she was educated to become a teacher. And his limited spare time was spent in becoming a self-taught plumber, a mechanic, and a handy man, whilst she had learnt how to budget, to cook, to clean, to sew, and to mother. That last task had been the hardest of all. Married women could not continue to teach in her day, so having children meant she had to give up the job she had loved.

She had been a single child so *mothering* skills did not come easily to her. Some days she wanted to scream at the endless washing, cooking and feeding duties she had to engage in. She wanted to sit down with a new book and read well into the night. But, sadly, she never did that. She knew the youngest child was a very early riser and would leave a pathway of destruction in her wake if not supervised.

She sighed.

We were so far away from help, she thought. *There was no extended family near us to bring wisdom or calm over our threshold. No, we weathered all that life threw at us, and we did it together.*

Until that one time when she had stepped away from the hardship of their lives.

He was a tree lopper. And everyone in the street employed him in the summer of 1960. He was handsome, strong, with a huge mop of curly hair. At thirty-one, and with all the children in school or kindergarten she saw freedom in every step he took. There was a range of trees to be cut down or trimmed in the street. Their tree was to be totally removed, the tree had died. So he stayed in her life for a precious few days, and he stayed in the street for a precious few weeks. Just long enough for the two of them to have formed a relationship. She remembers again every moment of the time they spent together. Every moment of the time when he took her into the realms of love and ecstasy. And she remembers the day when his work finished and he did not return to the street.

She had felt such agony, and she had sunk into the depths of such despair that had her whole family worried about her. Her husband asked time and again if he could help to take her distress from her. How could she admit that someone had come into her life and had shown her something so exquisite, and had then taken it from her? She didn't have the heart to destroy his feelings and his loving tenderness. So she slowly dragged herself from the bottomless pit she had sunk into and began to rebuild her life.

Her husband's kindness spilled over her every day, and gradually she began to respond with something of her old self. A pattern emerged between them. His was quiet devotion to her, and she returned to her bubbly self. The children were rewarded by her enthusiastic self. They were glad she was "back to normal".

Their life revolved around their daily occupations, the odd trip away, and then the new families emerged as each child found their niche in life, and partners to help them in these new roles. Life continued like this until the weekend away that she and her husband took to spend in the Forests of Frew. It was only about two hours drive from their home, and the hotel was pleasant, the food home-cooked, and the company relaxed.

Her husband sat down, watching her as she sat at the dresser, brushing her long hair, now shades of white and silver. And she smiled at him.

He started to speak, and as he did so, her face turned ashen, and the hairbrush slipped from her fingers. He started by saying "How I have loved these older years with you, my darling. Your company is what I long for at the end of each day. The completeness I feel with you I have never been able to express in words but I have tried so hard to show you."

And here he paused before continuing. "Do you know all those years ago when our tree was removed and you fell in love with *him*, I all but died. I couldn't compete with his charm, his physical beauty and his energy. And I saw the way his eyes followed you everywhere you went. I felt bereft when he found the way to your heart. I hurt in a way I have never known before. Then I ached for you when he left and you were just as bereft as me. I would have given anything to have been the one you showed that depth of feeling towards, and I could do nothing to help you, or myself."

He paused again before continuing. "It took weeks for each of us to heal, but we did, didn't we. And we found a different kind of love, and for that I am grateful. These older years have been some of the happiest times in my life."

She shook with shock. "You knew?"

"Yes, I knew" he replied. "From the moment he walked into our house, I knew. But he left, and you stayed. And you have never been unfaithful to me again so I learned that I could forgive because not to forgive would have meant I would have lost you completely. Anna, I couldn't have borne that, you meant so much to me."

And with that he slid to the floor, just two weeks shy of his 90th birthday. A man who had kept such a secret for a lifetime of years. A man with the charity to forgive her, and the ability to love her.

A small tear accompanied her reminiscing as she remembered holding him to her in those last precious moments of his life.

She adjusts the chair, lost again in her picture book of memories and the times she has learned to treasure. And a little sigh escapes her lips. "How lucky I was," she murmurs, to no one at all.

CR

Tiny Tales

Tiny drops
Falling gently
Onto pillow
Caravan leaks
Drama Day

Pedals pushed perfectly
Motors murmur musically
Bicycle breathes busily
Bliss

Pen poised
Thought died
Brain blank
Writer's block
Distraction needed

❧

Sister Mary Ursula

When she entered the convent, she was Joy Maloney, her birth name. But that quickly changed. The Mother Superior gave her the name of Sister Mary Ursula and she became one of the youngest novices in the cloistered convent, having gone straight from school to the convent. Her worldly knowledge was non-existent, matched only by her lack of experience, but she found her niche in the convent gardens. Throughout her novitiate, she took solace in the company of nature.

Sadly, this proved to be her undoing. The life of solitude, rescued only by the communication hour they had after tea, left her within herself and too afraid to come out. Her withdrawal went unnoticed by the other nuns used to the quietness of their youngest member.

And so it was that Sister Mary Ursula began her spiritual life with the Archangel Gabriel. She created him, she conversed with him, she took his guidance, even though at times he resembled her late father, she did not notice this. Her father had been a tower of a man. The voice of authority, kind, but not one to be crossed, he had been a strong influence in her life. Her mother was the perfect foil for him. She bounced from task to task, a little too busy for Joy. Not enough time in the day to devote special time to her only child. She had to be busy with the needs of Joy's father. And weren't they lucky to have such a man as a provider for them? And that had been the pattern of her life. She was seen but not heard.

The convent life became an extension of her home life. Seen but not heard. So she created her own world, and the Archangel Gabriel spread his large wings over her. He told her what to do, what to plant, where to be, until slowly her psyche became the Archangel Gabriel, and Joy diminished into nothingness.

It took two years for the other nuns to realise that something was seriously wrong with Sister Mary Ursula, and by then she could not retrieve reality; she had become truly insane.

Her small amount of possessions were placed in a suitcase. She left in an ambulance for the Psychiatric Hospital. Here she was put into the care of the Hospital's Chief Psychiatric Specialist. She had no idea her treatment came from the most dedicated of men. She was medicated; she had daily regimes created for her; patient plans were commenced, then later discarded. Other plans were commenced for her, and staff tried every form of reality orientation with her, but nothing worked.

The Archangel Gabriel would take over patient meetings, talk over the doctors; make demands of the gardeners, and bestow blessings on the nursing staff.

The cleaners and the kitchen staff received the holiest of all the blessings for the work they did. The Archangel Gabriel definitely had a "thing" about work. But no treatment for her worked. Sister Mary Ursula had morphed into the Archangel Gabriel and no medication was about to change that.

Over the months, she mellowed. The rants became less, although the blessings increased. Seasons came and seasons went. Staff accepted the Archangel Gabriel in their midst, and patients paid her little attention. She was once again seen but not heard.

Finally, one spring day, the staff sat down to discuss the entire case of Sister Mary Ursula. Her notes were comprehensive. They detailed her earlier life, her convent life, and her years in hospital. They knew she had become an institutionalised patient. The staff conceded they had given up on ever believing she could exist in a real world. The closest she came to reality was eating meals. Her clothing was changed for her, and her hygiene needs were endured by her. Staff kept a generalised routine for her, but for the most part, she kept to one or two niche areas where she prayed. Her medication was slowly decreased until it was no longer given. She never complained, she never answered to her given names, and although not the usual treatment for delusional patients, she was called Gabriel, to which she answered.

The situation would have stayed that way except for the illuminated thinking of the bright new Charge sister, who instigated the revue of patients with a long history of years in the hospital. She had a simple idea. When it was proposed to the senior staff members, the positive response set a course of action in progress.

First the Mother Superior of the Convent was asked to come into the hospital for the plan to be outlined to her. Her approval needed to be sought.

The plan was simple. Sister Mary Ursula was to be returned to the cloistered community at the convent after eight years as a hospital patient. She would receive no further treatment unless her condition deteriorated. She considered herself the Archangel Gabriel and was unlikely to ever return to her normal self, but in the religious, prayerful conditions of the convent she would be spiritually comforted, and at least there she would be accepted.

The Mother Superior asked many questions and all were answered. She understood what was being asked of the other nuns and of her. And she also understood that Sister Mary Ursula would be going "home". She would be cared for by those who understood her best.

And so it was that Sister Mary Ursula returned to the cloistered life. She returned to nature, to the garden, to the comfort of prayer, and to the understanding community of nuns with whom she had begun her journey into adulthood. She left the hospital in her Nun's habit, immaculate in her dress, and vacant in her eyes.

She was never seen in public again.

 C3

Lilibet
Beautiful name
Grandmother proud
Big brother to protect her.

C3

Success

Peter stood 6 feet 4 inches in his socks. His frame reflected strength and dominance, yet he rarely used this to gain what he wanted. He preferred to use his other attributes for that. He was well-versed in charm, with a quick and easy smile to accompany his requests. He was the man who got what he wanted with ease … until the day he met Susanne at Jimmy's housewarming party. She glowed with fresh, healthy beauty, and her musical voice captured his attention from the moment he walked onto the patio, observing the gathering of males in attendance. So he asked his mate to give him some background information on her.

"Sassy," said Jimmy, "intelligent, founded the start-up business Feet First. That's the one where you hike into all kinds of wilderness, experience Mother Nature, and she guides you home," adding, "She could guide me anywhere!"

So Peter waited, moving easily among the guests, a smile here and a word there, until much later, when he saw the guests beginning to take their leave, he made his move. He sauntered over to Susanne and introduced himself. He gave her his million-dollar smile and asked her about herself and then about her business. She answered him with the self-assuredness of a woman who knew where she was going in the world.

He listened, commented and engaged her then finally asked for her telephone number and with a laugh she gave him her card.

He left a little later himself because he believed that you always left them wanting a little more, made them keener, and he had plenty of time.

His financial business kept him busy for the next few days, but towards the weekend, he took her card from his wallet and called her. He was in the mood for a hunting weekend and he enjoyed the role of hunter.

No, sorry, she wasn't free this weekend.

So he bided his time and called again the following week. Once, again, she wasn't free. This time, he was a little surprised but he made a date with her for the following Friday. They would meet in a little Tapas and Wine Bar in the centre of town. Friday came, and she dropped him a quick message on his phone – something had come up, and she couldn't make the evening; could she postpone until the following Friday? He acquiesced feeling rather put out at the late change in plans.

Now he was eager to see her, and remembering how attractive she was, his days seemed to be longer with each hour. He conjured up a mental picture of her and went online to see her web page, finding another and more sharply focused photo of her advertising the Business. She was indeed quite beautiful. *Vivacious but attainable*, he told himself, although his hunting was never usually as prolonged as this.

Friday came and he waited in the Tapas and Wine Bar at 6pm, and she arrived, punctual to the minute. She carried a black gown that was draped over her arm and the sleek black suit she was wearing.

"Sorry," she said, "just rushed out from Court … didn't have time to change but didn't want to be late. How are you?"

He tried to reconcile the Court, the black garment and the Feet First Business, and came up with confusion. She caught the look on his face, and laughed.

"Oh," she said, "I thought you knew. Jimmy always introduces me as a businesswoman. Well, I am that, but only part-time. I'm a District Court Judge first, and that always takes precedence. And yes, I did have you checked out. I have to; my job depends on who I associate with. Well, so far in the checks and balances, you seem to have made the cut. So, what are we going to order?"

☙

The Benefactor

He wore the mantle of a normal man, like a cloak that allowed him to blend in with the man on the street. But the mantle was a façade that he used. He had cloaked himself in this since his inheritance had come through. The vast amount of money left to him by his uncle was known only to his accountant and himself. He wanted it that way.

Not for him the trappings of wealth, the jewellery, the electric car, the fine clothes. No, he was content with what he had. His only nod towards his wealth had come when he retired early from work. His colleagues were a little puzzled at him retiring at the age of sixty.

But he had retired to concentrate on the new job, one he had given himself.

It had all started some years back, the day he stopped in the park and had amused himself watching a small family on the swings and slides – a mother and two children full of laughter and joy. They tossed around love like it was a large rubber ball, each catching it and passing it on. They were kind to other little players at the park, and there was sharing of a small bag of lollies. Yet he could tell their clothing spoke of handed-down clothes. Nothing was new, and some of it was ill-fitting. It had not changed the children as they shared what they had and as their mother pushed the swings a little higher when it was their turn.

His captivation with the family had made him return to the park several times that week. They were often there and never once had he heard her raise her voice to the children. They had opened a small brown paper bag with sandwiches and had eaten their meagre lunch without complaint, returning to the slides, helping one another up the steps. Another day there was no food, but there were no complaints.

He watched the young and kind mother as she showed the children how to respect the playmates that came and went. She was always there for them, with arms that hugged and a voice that told them to try again. And he learned their names, Jack and Megs, as she called to them to come and see the ants' nest she found, telling them to watch the hard work the ants were doing. She dropped a few crumbs near the nest as they stared at the army of workers that retrieved the crumbs and bundled them off to their nest. He watched her tuck their hands in hers and he even followed her early one evening as she took them to the Fish and Chip shop, and allowed them to choose their treat for dinner.

He noted her down-at-heel shoes and the well-worn carry-everything bag she had with her, and then and there, he decided to share the benefits of his working life. She would thereafter get a sum of money weekly through a confidential source, and all he wanted in return was a summary of how it was spent. That was how he came to know she was a single mother, and how every cent he sent to her was used to create a home for the two children. He did notice in the park that the children's shoes were replaced with brand-new delightfully coloured shoes. And that caused him to smile.

So when his uncle died and left him as his sole heir, he viewed the money as a job. How would he get this money to those whose needs were as great as those of the precious mother and two children he had supported?

He wasn't quite sure how to do this when one night, as he watched the TV, an accident caught his eye. A family left without their father in the most tragic of circumstances. So he rang his accountant. And that became the pattern of his life – the new job he took on. There were so many tragedies that happened, so many families to whom he could give support. He spoke with his accountant, and between them, they set up a system that enabled him to channel money into those he saw in need of help. Sometimes, it was a one-off gift. Other times it was ongoing. But he always told his accountant to tell them that it would not last forever. His gift would only take them through the worst patch, perhaps up to two years, but not longer. After that, he expected they would have the confidence to start again.

He enjoyed the reports of the clever uses his money was put towards. The very first mother in the park had gone on to do a Nursing degree. And he knew she had married soon after. She was set, her life now on a path to success so his giving slowly ceased.

But what he didn't know was that their paths were destined to cross once more.

He had turned in his bathroom to reach for the towel when his foot slipped on a small puddle of water. An ambulance, the hospital, and surgery to straighten his broken leg saw him wheeled into Ward 4, the orthopaedic ward. He was hoisted gently onto the bed, his leg the recipient of pillows and support. The nurse at his side with pain relief in a small kidney dish looked so familiar that he looked again through his tired and pain-filled eyes. Was it the mother he had shared his salary with? Was it the mother of Jack and Megs?

He always asked for her when she was on shift, and he asked her so many questions about her life that he could have written her life story. He asked her to tell him over and over about the money she had received when she was so desperate for help and how, like a miracle, it had come. Regularly, week after week. And how she had never known who had been her benefactor.

He had a meeting with his accountant, and reset his will. Why he did that when he did, no one will ever know. But the blood clot that travelled from his break and eventually to his brain, took his life in the simplest of ways.

And she would never have known of his earlier generosity had it not been for the accountant who summoned her to his rooms. With the beauty of the giver to the most worthy of recipients, he had told her she was now debt-free. There was a condition though. She had to continue his client's good work. His client had thought she would come across so many people less well off than herself; she would be able to continue the distribution of his monies. Was she able to accept the money under those conditions?

The tears that flowed down her face seeped past her answer as she replied yes.

The child she gave birth to six months later was christened after her benefactor. At the christening, she told her benefactor in a quiet whisper, "Your name shall be a part of this family all the days of my life, Oscar Peter Williams."

☙

The Brothel

Jenny had lived in a brothel for all the years she could remember. Her mother had run the brothel from the age of twenty. She had recruited a group of women, many of whom she had rescued from the streets. They were grateful for the food, shelter, and a warm bed, and their loyalty to her was strong.

Even after some had left to marry or travel, most of them stayed in touch. She, Jenny, had regarded these women as aunts, or as she got older, she thought of them as sisters. She herself had never worked in her mother's brothel. No, her mother had insisted she get a good education, and she had eventually studied law and completed her degree, which had pleased all the aunts and sisters she had.

She occasionally worked as the receptionist for her mother when they were particularly busy, as happened when the race meetings were on, or the charity marathons, or some pop star was entertaining in town. This, her mother had been grateful for. None of the women begrudged her the fact that she had done well; in fact, they came to rely on her for legal advice. She smiled at the thought of the Pro Bono work she did, and the scrapes she extricated so many of the women from. Her situation might have seemed bizarre to many but it seemed quite normal to her.

But she had begun to realise that she needed now to move on, to commence her own practice. So, taking a leaf from her enterprising mother, she engaged others who specialised in areas in which she was less proficient. And that was how she came to employ a commercial lawyer aptly named Prudence. And what followed on from that became a truly remarkable story.

Prudence shared many a visit to Jenny's mother's home, and her interest was piqued in what the women did with their earnings. Some were supporting a family; some were single mothers supporting children, and some just spent their earnings as they received it.

Prudence decided that, with a little influential help from Jenny, she could turn these women's money into thousands more. She began to run classes with them; she taught them how to invest in reliable companies and to sell when the markets were favourable. She showed them the best investments available, and she made sure that any financial wizard who came to share their sexual wares also gave them information that could be used to benefit all of the women. She safeguarded their investments and showed them the evidence of their investments on a six-monthly basis.

The girls took to this enterprise with vigour. The financial advisors who frequented the establishment found their pillow talk informative and knowledgeable, and exchanges of information happened almost on a daily basis.

Jenny's mother began to take part in the lessons and many an evening was spent in doing a review of incomes earned.

Word got around that this was one brothel that could give extras, but not the normal kind of extras. For the men, they thrived on the sex and investment promotion. For the women, they thrived on the earnings from the sex and the investment opportunities. It was indeed a very satisfactory reciprocal arrangement.

Jenny's mother never charged anything for those extras that her girls were providing because the benefits flowed naturally into her coffers. Little by little, the women began to buy homes for themselves and then homes to use as rentals and income. Some chose to leave at this point, mostly to raise their families, while others stayed because the lifestyle was familiar to them.

Between Jenny and Prudence, they began to set up trust funds, companies, and enterprises that were discussed with the women, agreed to by all, and were indeed profitable. All taxes were paid. All was done completely within the law. Although the girls often laughed at what they called Insider Information, or Insider trading. The joke was a pithy one and could bring them all undone with laughter.

The swinging sign outside the premises may have read *The Chef's Delight*, but in reality, that was only the entrée. The main meal was the *Women's Investment Society*.

And, as unlikely as it might have seemed, the team of Jenny and Prudence also brought about other changes in the brothel. The Sports Room changed, depending on the season. It alternated between being a Cricket Room, bowling a maiden over, to a football room with tries and goals. The girls entered into the fun. They learned the Club songs and could sing the chorus of all sixteen AFL club songs. Grand Final night became a legend at the brothel and it brought the other activities to a standstill while they all watched the best teams in the competition fight it out for the Cup.

The brothel acquired some trophies of its own, and they were signed and framed and hung in the entranceway – collectors' items that would eventually be worth a considerable amount of money as the years passed. They even had an annual trophy of their own, but for other interesting abilities, usually awarded to the player with the greatest stamina. Of course, the winner could only have his first name engraved on the plaque; no judge or politician or media personality could afford to have both names printed on the silver shield.

Jenny noticed the earnings from the Round Room were greater than the earnings from the other rooms. She said it had to be because there was the element of chase involved in the outsized gigantic round bed. And the Bondage Room was enhanced by creating a Police Cell with a Judge's stand and gavel. "By order of the Court!" was heard down the passageways as the gavel was thumped into its stand. The men loved it. It became a real money spinner. The police had no need to search the premises for anything illegal, but their visits were "for observation" and to keep the brothel staff "safe," they said. Jenny's mother allowed them their fantasies.

It was decided to start a small shop within the brothel, and many were the wives and girlfriends who benefitted from the items on sale. They were always packaged like a present, with bows and cards, but nothing with a name that indicated from where they had been bought.

And you might be forgiven for thinking that something or someone would come along to wreck the ingenious enterprises of the women, but you see it didn't. The Me Too movement in the brothel protected them all financially, and, ultimately, physically and emotionally.

They grew older together, the younger ones maintaining the patrons, the older ones maintaining the brothel and the Sunshine Coast retreats they all used. They even decided to have a Home for the retired prostitutes, complete with nursing staff and entertainment, and thinking of a name for it became the highlight of the year, until finally one of them came up with the title:

The ICloud; a play on words, but so apt.

As Jenny and Prudence said on their retirements, now they were all entering into a highly different world. Technology. This was definitely going to be the new era, for clients and staff. And weren't the girls going to make some money out of the robotic inventions.

What an exciting thought. They mentioned the spa baths with automatic body blow dries. The moving beds, the robotic assistants, the massagers, and here they ran out of ideas as they walked up the gangway into the Cruise ship. A little reward they had given themselves for their dedication to the menu of *The Chef's Delight*, and all its patrons. Tonight, they would toast the patrons, every last one of them, from whom they had made a considerable fortune and they would smile at the bank balances of the incredible women they had taught.

Aaah, it was a woman's world indeed.

ℝ

The Card Game

The six of them sat down to play. The table had the Card cloth on it now that the meal was finished. The serious time was approaching.

Now, the Men always played the Women in this group. They had done it for years, and so were accustomed to it. They all knew their seating arrangements, who sat on which side of whom. That was important because you never sat on either side of your husband. That way you could drive home at the end of the evening and, win or lose, you could discuss the game and still enjoy your spousal relationship.

In the early days, the men used to brag about how they had won the time before, which was really a figment of their combined imaginations. So, to save this from being a constant irritation, an exercise book now kept all the scores, and the winner's rights were there in black and white. It was true that the Men had won the greater percentage of games, but that figure was being constantly whittled down by the Women.

And so, the serious side of the evening commenced.

The Card game was Pony Canasta. The most difficult form of Canasta.

You played with two hands of cards, one which you held in your hand and one which you had to earn. That hand was kept face down on the table until such time as the rules permitted you to pick it up and add it to your hand. That was one of the objectives of the game, to acquire the "Pony", and to do this early so you could make points for your team.

The conversation flowed. What were every family's children up to? Well, not children, really; they were all mature adults, many with children of their own. But an update was called for. Something important may have occurred in the six weeks between games. So, families and their fortunes and misfortunes were shared, and solace given or praise proclaimed. (Depending on the most recent information.)

As the game moved on, the odd piece of criticism flew over the table, like: Why did you play that card? Or: You let them get the pack, now we're in trouble. Oh yes, it was deemed appropriate to make your feelings known if one of your partners played well or conversely if they played with ridiculous non observance of the cards that had preceded theirs. It certainly was expected that you would follow the play of all other card players. And whether or not the Women or the Men won, partners were hi-fived, or shot eyeball daggers at from close range.

The relationships survived because, as the years passed, everyone had come to the same conclusion: no one was playing for "sheep stations," as the expression goes. You might lose this night and win the next. No one carried grievances. So the grimaces when a bad card was played, and the delighted good humour that was exhibited when a good play was masterfully accomplished was all part of the evening.

The evening always started with a meal shared. The games were held at a different home each time, and the recipes tried out on the players were many and varied. The critique of the food was always the same. Brilliant, mainly because two couples had not had to prepare it, or to clean up or wash up afterwards. And that was an evening made in heaven.

You laboured when it was your turn, but hey, that only came around once every eighteen weeks. The night when one couple cooked everything, you might have enjoyed as a child was a night made for children, albeit grown-up children. The finishing touch being the Golden Syrup Pudding with lashings of cream. And that caused a lot of reminiscing over foods enjoyed as a child. Then there was the night another couple cooked with great Asian Flair, different tastes, different spices and all consumed by the appreciative audience. Of course, wine accompanied the meal, and may have been the reason why (on the odd occasion) there was the unfortunate misplay of cards, when really you should have known better. But all was forgiven before the last goodbyes were called as the cars departed.

There was one habit the menfolk had begun at some stage in the development of the Card Evenings. Partway through the evening, they would all depart to speak to one another outside while examining the lemon tree. Every couple had a lemon tree, and the guys watered it with great gusto regardless of the weather. Unless it was raining of course. Like the football players who get into a huddle to make decisions about a winning play so too did the three men. They would return with a conspirator look on their faces after their "time out", followed by a "now we've got you" expression.

It actually began to irritate the three women, this wait and let them conspire something over at the Lemon tree. They said little, just sat and scowled, until the most memorable night when one of the women said into the waiting void.

"Ladies, I'm about to deal. What cards would you like? If the guys want to make us wait for them and their conferences, let's make the most of it. What would you like me to give you?"

And so it was that, when the Men returned and sat down, they picked up a set of cards very carefully composed by the Women. The Women's cards were likewise very carefully composed. And it was on for young and old. The Women scored mightily, picked up the pack off the Men several times, their card hands flowed like they were set up to flow, which indeed they were. The Men grouched at their lack of good cards, played on and went further and further down the beaten track. The score at the end of that hand was sufficient to take the Women to complete victory. The evening was won.

The strange thing about all of this was the Women didn't own up to what they had done for about two years. They just lived off the night when they had won handsomely and thoroughly and refused to let the Men forget it. It was the talk of the town, so to speak, at each and every card game for at least a year. *The magnificent card game the Women had played, the cleverness with which they had added to their partner's hands. The score which they had accrued, which was one of the best of that year.*

No, they stayed mum about it and let the Men know that they were not to be trifled with, and don't raise the "I think we won last time" issue again. For the next few months, the menfolk were subdued, and there were several more times that the Women crashed through all their defenses and took out the crown for the evening. Funnily enough, there was never a word spoken about it by the Women for about two years thereafter. It was as though, by mutual and unspoken agreement, they colluded in silence about their actions.

They loved being able to quietly remind the guys that the Women were a team to be reckoned with, and no mistake.

Then came the evening when one of the Women, still talking about "that game", with a wink and a nod at the other two, admitted to the combined conspiracy.

The three Women looked at the Men, who could utter not one word. "We just got tired of you three going outside to conspire against us, and we thought we would teach you a lesson. We thought well fairs fair. You talk about your conquering actions; we'll just do our conquering actions."

Still the menfolk sat in stunned silence.

Now the outcome of *that* evening was transformative.

The lemon tree was left in peace, and the cards shuffled and dealt only when all six persons were present. And so it remains to this day. And yes, the Card evenings are still ongoing – it's a little bit like *in sickness and in health until death do us part*, the six turn up with great gusto all set for another beautiful meal, and a combative evening of cards. And *That* evening is never mentioned. Except when the Women are alone and they roar with laughter at their marvellous duplicity and the fun they had that night.

◌ↄ

Innocence

"Do you go to school, Nana?"
Tiny tot at Kindy door.

Precious

Bucket-loads
of tears.
"Blankie" flew out car window.

Grandmothers

Women in Aqua Class
"Nana," voice calls.
All heads turn.

Modern Mum

In-tray overloaded
Desk overloaded
Filing on floor
"Bored?" unknown word.

World map

Longing eyes.
World map
Passport filed.
Virus rampant!

The Duchess

By Society scorned
by family failed
but,
by Harry loved.

☞

The Flasher

If I have had three similar experiences in one lifetime, multiplied by all the women in society – good grief there are a lot of exhibitionists out there.

You need me to explain that opening sentence, don't you.

My first experience of a "Flasher" was in my secondary school years.

As a group of teenagers walking down the short street to our school, we managed to acquire a Flasher, only back then I didn't know that was what they were called. A man, reasonably dressed, would wait until two or three girls passed him, and then, with delight and ceremony, he would expose his what we called back in those days "private parts".

Since we were young and very inexperienced convent girls, he frightened the heck out of us all. But he obviously got a thrill out of it because he kept this up for a week, and for pure shock value he made a killing. He got responses of all sorts. Squeals, screams, fright, and girls running for the sanctity of the school. I never knew if the police caught him because they didn't ask me to appear as a witness.

Since I came from a home with two brothers and a dad, I simply thought the guy was stark-raving mad.

The second time it happened, I was a little older, and a lot more aware. But it still took me by surprise. By then, I had worked in general and psychiatric hospitals, and nothing about the male's shape or size surprised me. I had even had the dubious pleasure of having to dress a delicate area for a farmer who had shot the end off his delicate self while he was cleaning a gun. Who cleans a loaded gun? Just saying.

Now, that will make most men cringe, to say the least. For the nursing staff, it was a labour of love for the most unfortunate gentleman who died a thousand deaths each time the dressing was renewed. Nobody laughed when the tears rolled down his face in agony.

However, as an adult, when walking from the Central Railway station in Sydney en route to a particular shop and fairly self-absorbed, I passed a car parked by the walkway. And you guessed it, there he was on display. What on earth! Was my expression. Oh, good grief. For all the world to see, middle of the afternoon with women and children passing by.

What an idiot. I could have been an off-duty policewoman. I decided not to give him the satisfaction of seeing my face in fits of laughter and kept walking. Silly me, I should have called the Police. But it was funny.

Then, at a mature age and teaching mature students, I personally took a class of them to the Perth District Courts. They had a set project and, like a lot of university courses, were expected to do some external classwork. I knew that in the courts on a Monday morning, there was always a parade of the flotsam and jetsam of life. It came after the weekend of petty criminal activity of many of our fellow Perth residents.

Into the Court came a gentleman dressed in a three-piece suit. His blue waistcoat matched his blue suit. His shoes were shining from polish. A dapper tie completed the ensemble.

His name was called. He stepped forward as the charge was read to him. My class of students either smiled or smothered giggles, as the charge read out by the police officer was: Sitting in the boot of his car, lid up, at the Dog Beach down by Scarborough Beach, exposing himself to all the female dog owners taking their pets on their morning walk to the beach.

My face must have said it all. My brain was saying *He sat in his own car, doing this, with his own number plate on the car, which of course any smart female would memorise as she rang the police.* In today's world, they would simply take a photo of it, of course. The number plate that is, and yes, she might have added a more personalised photo for good measure.

Now here he was in court, dressed like he was about to go to a very important meeting, and having to plead Guilty as Charged to a crime that would be recorded for all the world to see, forever.

I then found myself wondering how I would take the next class as they analysed the behaviour they witnessed in court. But the thing about teaching mature-aged students is that you can relax with them and have a good belly laugh with them as they look at the sheer idiocy of the gentleman in the three-piece suit. And we did—all of the above.

I know this lesson was filled with interaction, laughter, wise cracks, and a lot of good humour. And I thank "him" for making this a lesson they wouldn't forget. A picture tells a thousand words, so I really didn't have to say much. The students got the message.

But as I wrote at the beginning: three public episodes in one lifetime. If every woman had this number of misadventures, they would have to believe that the male of the species has a segment of brain that he isn't using.

૏

The Key

It had rusted somewhat but it still hung in the same place. It was the key to nowhere. Well, at least that's what I had always thought. Not the most usual of keys, it had been hung inside the horse shed on a large nail by my father. I remember questioning him about its existence.

"What does it unlock? Why is it there?" I had said to him, inquisitive as 7-year-olds are. And I always received the same answer.

"Could be the key to heaven you know," he would say. So it became a game with us. The key to heaven – 'no, not using it today,' he would say as he brushed down the mare before letting her out into the paddock. Or he might say, 'not ready for heaven yet, are we, but we've got the key when we need it.'

So I made up stories about what it would unlock, and when we sat down to have our morning tea after feeding time with the horses, I would tell my dad about what that key was going to unlock. They were all fanciful stories, and when I was younger, they included fairies and wands and the like. As I grew older, the stories took on a life of their own, and I would imagine what this key could unlock, the secrets it would expose.

Dad listened and would smile, a very knowing smile, and he would tell me what a wonderful imagination I had. And then, one day, he became really serious and said perhaps I should collect all these stories together and tell them to the world.

And just like that, my writing career began. I wrote essays, stories, and assignments, and that solidified my wish—I wanted to become a journalist. I wanted to tell the world my stories. English was easy for me, and writing was second nature to the teenage me, like the free-flowing stream that bounded our property.

But journalism has a way of taking you from country to country and there was a period of time when I was never home. Dad and I would talk by phone as he checked that I was not in a danger zone in some far-off place. I would reassure him and then quietly put on my bulletproof vest and hard hat and mingle with the soldiers in yet another war. I would write until the sun came up telling my stories to the world and sending the dispatches back to the papers I was syndicated to.

So, wandering and watching and writing became my life, and perhaps it might have remained so but I received a message from my dad's brother to tell me Dad needed me. He was ill, and the fastest plane home would only just be soon enough.

I sat by his bed and tried to understand what it was that he was so concerned about, and then I finally got it. The key. He wanted me to get the key. Was I really going to find the answer to all those childhood questions, what the key would actually unlock? And some box he kept in the loft … was that what he was asking for?

I went back to the farm for that key. The now rusted thing still hung in the shed on a nail. I climbed into the loft and found a box sitting under the eaves. I took them back to the hospital and put them gently into his gnarled old hands. And he whispered to me to come closer. He tried the key in the keyhole of the box, and because it was so rusted it took several turns before it gave way and opened.

And there inside was a photo album filled with pictures, faithfully stored in now curled, old plastic sleeves. Picture after picture of myself, as a baby, a two-year-old, a three-year-old, and later some pictures that I hadn't even known he had taken.

He looked at the pictures and said so softly I could barely hear him, "The gift that I was given from Heaven — the company, the love, the hugs — so much, so much."

Slowly, his voice trailed off, and the pictures slipped from his hands. I realised that the bond that had been created in those early days had been the keys to his heart.

❧

One of the Seven Deadly Sins

The feelings of hatred bit deeply into him and he watched as the man emerged from the hairdressers with his new and sharply slicked haircut. He watched as the man crossed the road to hail a taxi to return him to work. His immaculate suit, his crisp white shirt reflecting the light, and his silk tie swinging, his briefcase under his arm, his air of confidence emanating from every step he took.

There was nothing pure about hatred. Only that it was an all-consuming emotion. It pervaded his thoughts and his actions. He pulled the ragged coat a little closer to him to keep out the cold that seeped through his thin underclothes.

He came every fortnight to this hairdresser, just to glimpse the man on whom his hatred rested. He had done this for many months now. He wasn't recognised by anyone, his down-and-out appearance giving most city dwellers a reason to give him a wide birth, his ratty beard and uncut moustache acting like a camouflage.

Yet, once he had walked these streets … walked them as though he owned them. He called out to those who passed him with words of recognition and the joviality in his voice as they responded to his words, always giving his step an extra lift. He even had a nickname bestowed on him by the locals. Mr F, they called him. Standing for Mr Finance, because of his Midas touch. Everything he invested in turned to gold. He had city folk following his every financial lead, even the mother and father brigade accepted his knowledge. He was superb in his understanding of money, how to make it, how to spend it, and how to revel in it. Money, and the power that it brought him. The friends that it gathered to him, the people who wanted to be in his inner circle. He lived the life of a man of greatness.

At least he did, until he employed someone with an almost identical knowledge and drive as himself. Someone he trusted. Someone who he shared his resources with, and who he taught his skills to.

And that someone betrayed him. Used him. Gathered his information and sold him to the police while remaining the sole proprietor of his company. *His* company. The five years he'd spent behind bars deepened his desire for revenge on a daily basis. He built up an internal rage and plotted and replotted how he would take his wrath, his frustration and his anger out on his ex-partner after his release.

Finally, his release date came, and he had shuffled through the prison gates with his few personal belongings and a card giving him accommodation in a small cramped and unclean hovel. His possessions were meagre but his mind was full – full of the plan he had created. It was a timed, structured plan and one that there would be no coming back from. He could not enjoy the profits of his company, but before this month was through neither would his ex-partner.

ℭℜ

Retirement

"Let's have a serious discussion about housework now that we are retired," said Jenny's husband.

Well, for starters, he never had serious discussions about anything other than football, so this was a deviation from the norm.

"Once upon a time," he continued, "we both had defined work jobs, and home jobs. Now everything is supposed to be shared. And that's where all the confusion comes from. I mean I don't ask you to clean the car."

And that's true. He cleaned it, roughly, every six weeks or so. Rarely did he vacuum, or do the interior of the car but he kept the exterior of the vehicle clean. "And you shouldn't ask me to clean the house."

She thought: *But that's the daily chores. That's why I am so exhausted.*

"I look after the shed, and you should look after the inside of the house," he added.

She thought: *The shed is 10 foot by 10 foot, and in a constant state of dust, and difficult to find anything in it when needed. The house, on the other hand, is a three-bedroom, two-bathroom, two-studies home, with a family room to boot.*

She listened for a while longer to the illogical distribution of chores ... oh, the garden was hers, too, flowers and vegie patches and the patio because it was "a part of the house." In return, he would do the washing, not the ironing ... *funny that* ... and they would both be able to hang the washing out and bring it in. *Oh, so that meant he put the unsorted clothes into the machine and turned it on.*

The one-sided conversation came to an end. He was satisfied.

Somehow so many things got omitted. He had his own bathroom and toilet – sorry, that was part of the house. The kitchen was definitely her domain; after all, she used it the most. The irony of that went completely over his head.

She sat later and decided there had to be an answer for this. She was too tired at the end of each day for this to continue. So she made a plan. It was really quite a simple plan.

A gardener once a fortnight; a lawn mower guy once a month; two cleaners once a week; a window cleaner once a month; all ironing once a week, picked up, ironed and delivered back to the house; and Home Delivery of seven complete evening meal ingredients, with recipes, once a week.

Lunch and breakfast were not too arduous; she would do that. Well, mostly.

A Mr Fix-it guy once a month, she'd use the Hire-a-Hubby company – she had heard they were good – they did the small jobs, the touch-up of paintwork, and such.

Then she worked on her diary. Her lunches with friends (that was in place of TV sports for her). The occasional breakfast out by herself to try out various cafés. She'd keep a note of how good the facilities were.

The Seniors University Group, she had always wanted to play Mahjong, so she would enroll for the beginner's course. She would resume cards at the Bridge Club where she liked cards; Exercise groups, especially for the older people, yes! and Yoga to keep her supple. Throw in some Entertainment nights and her month looked like a happy and diverse one. Did she have suitable clothes for this new life? *No, perhaps not. Well, a little online shopping should fix that.*

And so it was.

Over the course of the next week, all was organised and set in place. At the start of October, the hired help arrived. She dismissed the incredulous looks he gave her. She didn't hear the requests for costings and ignored the request for receipts. She just paid them all.

The month of October, she caught up with friends, found her Mojo again, as she called it, wore her new clothes and left the labouring in the safe hands of those she employed. She was almost always home to cook the dinner, and decided that for the times when she was going to one show or another, she would just leave him a frozen meal.

October moved into November. And it continued. Protestations fell on deaf ears – hers anyway.

The house sparkled. She invited friends over, and she entertained. She went out daily; she had things to do and places to be and the smile never left her face.

The Bridge Club had led to a Pottery Group, and she excelled at making pottery. It took many hours of her time. The phone rang constantly as arrangements were made to collect her, or for her to be the driver. They took it in turns, you see.

And her life was full and happy.

He wondered why he felt the way he did. He wasn't included in many of her outings, and he certainly couldn't make pottery, or play Mahjong. He wasn't much good at cards, and she rarely went to the football with him anymore.

They ate dinner together in the early evenings but she always had something to do to prepare for the next day, so the rest of the evenings he spent on his own. He began to feel lonely. He missed her company, her enthusiasm, and being able to tell her about the football matches he watched on TV. That seemed to be his only occupation. She never growled at him for not doing a chore she had asked him to do. She just gave the chores to the hired help. Everything got done. The ceilings got repainted, the lights got refitted, the carpets cleaned, and the home help left the house immaculate each week. The dishwasher got emptied and cleaned; that was once a chore he had signed up for but had never gotten around to doing.

She was always immaculately dressed each day, not in ultra-chic clothing but appropriate, smart clothing, always ironed. She never even took the car each day; no, she left it for him, quite content to be picked up by friends or to take the bus. She knew all the bus routes and times.

And the hollowness inside him grew as the months passed. She was living, and he wasn't. She was living without him, and he didn't know how to live without her. He knew they had started out together, living so much of their lives together, and he realised that he had changed long before she had. He had settled into a life where he simply left it all to her … until one day she didn't, and she wouldn't. And she regained her life and momentum with the help of trades men, and gardeners, and clever small business firms.

And now his life was cold, and empty, and probably too late to be lived. And he realised that he had done all this to himself. With all-seeing eyes, he saw his future, and he realised that it contained almost nothing.

⳽

The Petulant Child

The dictionary defines *petulance* as an attitude belonging to a child, when a child is bad-tempered and sulky. Usually, because they have not been able to get their own way

Well, this was one bad-tempered and sulky child. And it was my misfortune to sit directly in front of said child on an aircraft with three hours flying time still to come.

This child, who was about five or six years old, whined, grizzled, argued, and flung himself about in his seat, hitting the back of mine constantly.

I debated slapping the legs that hit my seat but thought I might get a reprimand from the Air Hostesses. I did politely ask the mother to have the son cease and desist his actions, but he had a mind of his own, and his mother's words were ignored. In fact, he kicked my chair even more after she spoke to him.

I did wonder if the Air Hostesses might take him up to the cockpit and "show" him the flight deck but it was one of those flights where everything seemed to be going wrong. Not enough chicken, run out of salad sandwiches, that sort of thing, so they were scurrying back and forth and ignoring the petulant child.

Now I am not one to suffer in silence. No, I am productive with silence. In my silence, I was constructing a way of getting my own back on smarty pants behind me.

I went to the back of the plane and asked for a very large drink of water and another of ice blocks, and I slowly made my way back towards my seat. The arms were waving, and the legs were flying about, so it wasn't hard for me to have his legs come into contact with what I was carrying. Of course, the water went all over him, followed by the ice blocks.

I don't know who was more shocked, him or his mother. But at least it silenced him for one whole minute as he stared disbelievingly at his shirt front and small pants now completely sodden with water and ice. He opened his mouth to yell and I beat him to the "punch".

"Look what you made me do," I yelled at him. "Your mother told you to sit still, now just look at what has happened, and it's all your fault."

His bottom lip quivered, but not a sound came out of his mouth, but in the seats surrounding him, there was a clapping of hands.

I know I towered over him. At six and a half feet tall, I tower over a lot of people. And with my rather scruffy beard, grown long because I am on holiday, I must have looked a formidable sight. Not to mention my very deep voice which sounds quite like the proverbial foghorn. The "it's all your fault" was foghorns at their best.

Petulance: it is a very good word, very descriptive, but subdued is an even better word. And subdued he stayed until he fell asleep in his wet and miserable seat. And the rest of us … well, we had a relaxing flight home.

CR

The Soul

His soul wandered desolately through the cemetery, caught by the parameters of the graveyard, moving slowly from corner to corner, past monuments and gravestones, past flowers and ponds, doomed to be captive within the walls of the burial grounds of so many.

The history of the city could be traced through those who inhabited the sacred plots. The graves spoke of the farmers, the soldiers, the workers, the mothers, and occasionally those who had left this earth in the flowering of their youth. But their souls had risen to be rewarded for their well-lived lives, while he was condemned to stay aimless and wandering.

He knew he deserved this nothingness, this emptiness, this inability to touch or be touched, and this agony of floating incompleteness. He knew when the pathway of death had enveloped him that his life so badly lived was only worthy of condemnation. But he had not realised that his soul would be left in this eeriness of nothing. Without life, without purpose, condemned to this suspended state because he could no longer make reparation for the sins he had committed while he had inhabited the earth.

Day followed night followed day followed night as his soul touched the top of the tombstones, and the newly dug graves. As he watched, another coffin was slowly lowered into the ground. This was the same as before, the same as before, the same as before.

His soul drifted over his headstone and he read again, as he had done so many times before, John Timothy Smith. Born in

1960, Died in 2020. The few words inscribed on his bare stone.

No words that said loved son, or loved husband of, or father of. No vase of flowers tended lovingly, placed beside the etchings. The grass was cut by the workmen, not clipped by little sheers held tenderly by a loved one. No visitors stopped to gaze with affection at his gravesite nor say a prayer for him.

His gift to his community was nothing, and his sparsely worded gravestone reflected nothingness. His soul continued in its entrapment – the same as before.

A young girl entered the cemetery carrying a large bunch of flowers. She was followed by her mother. They walked towards the newest monument and, kneeling, began to arrange the flowers in a beautiful crystal glass vase, talking animatedly about the father and husband whose graveside they decorated. They prayed together and, holding hands, sang a lovely slow hymn over his grave as they placed a photo by the vase. The picture reflected three people. The husband, the wife, and the young girl, her arms around a large doll, her face alight with happiness.

When they had finished singing, the young girl looked over at his stark John Timothy Smith inscription, and the smile slid from her face, and a small tear escaped her eye. He watched the tear roll down her cheeks and onto her father's grave, and he wished he could feel those tears; he wished he could dry those tears, and his soul felt a torment he could not explain.

He watched them leave and his soul was heavy with regret for what he might have done, could have done, to have given of himself. He felt a longing for the love he saw in the young girl's eyes and the gentleness he saw in the mother's face. He wanted just to touch the tear that had escaped the little girl's eye.

His soul roved and roamed in its endlessness, but each time, it came back to the crystal vase with its scented flowers. He felt the love that surrounded the new mound of earth and the father whose remains lay beneath it.

The days and hours had no meaning to him; they were for the living. In this timeless place, he flew silently past the old and new gravesides, always weighed down by his emptiness.

The girl returned with her mother many times. Each time, she carried flowers, said a prayer, and sang a song, and then, as she was ready to leave, she turned her small head and read his gravestone again, and a single tear fell. He passed by her, moved around her, and, in agony, wanted to comfort her, but his nothingness stopped his every gesture.

His soul began to be filled with pain, and an indescribable effort to offer tenderness to the beautiful child he watched. And he could do nothing. His regrets poured over him in excruciating, enveloping waves of pain. His soul writhed at his complacent life, given to no one, helping no one, caring for no one, and his wretched soul began another circuit of the cemetery.

The mother and child came a little less often now to the father's graveside, and summer became autumn. He waited longingly throughout the seasons for the ritual they had created. He waited for the child to gaze with such sadness at his tombstone, and he knew that each time she looked, she would shed a tear for him.

Winter came, and with it, the cold days and fewer visitors to the gravesites. Now he waited and waited, his anxiety increasing the pain in his soul, and then, as a small patch of blue sky opened over her father's grave, he saw them come into the cemetery. How long had she been away, he couldn't measure time anymore, except by the deep and burning pain he felt.

As she walked in, rugged up in a coat and boots, he flew towards her to stop her slipping on the wet path. This time, her hands were full. She carried two bunches of flowers, and her mother carried another beautiful crystal glass vase, just like her father's vase. He watched with a longing his soul could not fill as she rearranged the new flowers into her father's vase, and then into the new vase. Quietly, she worked, and when satisfied, she asked her mother's approval, and her mother nodded.

She turned towards his headstone and carefully placed the second vase beside his name. This time, when they prayed, she included John Timothy Smith in her prayers, and the sweet rendition of Amazing Grace was directed at both of the graves. She sprinkled love over her father's grave, and somehow, amazingly, she sprinkled some on his.

And he felt a change in his soul, a lightness where it had been heavy, and a movement that lifted his soul as though the bonds that had kept it on earth were breaking and his soul began to lift out of the cemetery. As it moved, it began a gentle ascent towards the light above, the ever-enfolding light of eternity, and as he looked back behind him, he promised the little girl he would look after her. *For every precious tear you shed for me there will be a thousand times my wings will guide you and my love will protect you,* he prayed over her, and this time as he watched not a single tear fell from her eyes. Instead, she looked first from the tombstone, then towards the blue sky that crept through the clouds, and a little smile played around her lips.

As his soul was enveloped by the soothing light, it began to sing.

The seasons came and went, and the years gathered husbands and children and the young girl grew to womanhood. Marked in her diary were the dates of her mother's and father's deaths, and the death of John Timothy Smith, and every year she paid the three gravesites a visit.

The vases had long since been replaced, but the flowers were always fresh and the sites were carefully tended. She still prayed and sang over their bodies, and occasionally her daughter would visit with her. She had explained to her daughter that she had adopted John Timothy Smith, and when she explained to her family that he had been her protector all her life long, no one quite knew what to make of it.

How could she ever have explained his presence, the felt presence she had of him? How could she explain that when the gentle zephyr enveloped her, she knew he held her protectively? How could she ever explain that she knew he was in pain and that, in her youth, she knew he needed prayers and love?

But she had known – she had known her young and innocent soul talked with his soul. They had met over scented flowers in a graveyard, and they had completely understood each other.

She showed him her love and allowed him to show his regret for the uselessness of a life lived without generosity and kindness. And in the melting of his heart grew love, tenderness, and caring. From this small child, he had learned what it meant to be loved and to love. His arms remained open for the day and the time when he would share his reward with her.

CЯ

The Ticket

She smiled quietly to herself although her heart was racing. Not a flicker on her face betrayed the emotion she was feeling. She quietly let herself out of the house and walked towards the bus stop. He thought she was going to the local library but she had a far different destination in mind. She took the bus into the town and headed towards the Lottery Office. Once inside she walked to the counter and noticed how everyone smiled at her. Every face behind the counter looked happy. But not as happy as she was, no sir. She placed the ticket on the counter and asked politely for it to be checked.

The counter staff came back with the broadest of smiles, repeatedly saying congratulations to her. 'First prize,' they said. 'How marvellous for you.' And looking down at her dowdy shoes and Red Cross coat she knew she didn't look the picture of wealth, well not right now anyway.

They took her into a small room and she realised that this was where they would counsel her, telling her how to put the money into some safe bank account. Actually, she didn't need that. She had a complete plan worked out and safety was a priority for her.

She simply gave them a Bank account name and number and asked for the money to be placed there immediately. Within seconds it was done. She declined the offer of advice and assistance, and the well-meant words telling her to just wait, do nothing until the joy of being wealthy beyond her wildest dreams had sunk in.

She thought to herself she had spent this money in her head at least a thousand times; now all she was doing was actually spending it. The account she had placed the money into required only one signature to withdraw amounts of money – hers. For twenty-five years she had been on the receiving end of a husband whose control of money had shrivelled her until there was no love left for him. He had handed out small portions, always demanding to see receipts, never allowing her to buy anything that he deemed frivolous. Not for her the smart shoes, the neat slacks, the cosy jumpers. No, she shopped in the Red Cross and accepted the seconds as though they were gifts. She had made do; she had restitched the garments and had tried her best to look fashionable with the meagre wardrobe she had. But this was to be a thing of the past.

She sat down at the coffee shop and ordered a large latte, and sipped it, then ordered one of the beautiful brownies she had often coveted as she had walked past this gay and happy café. She realised she would have to put all of her ideas into place slowly.

The first thing she was going to do was to buy herself a flat on the other side of town, one in the new tower block that overlooked the lake. She would have it furnished by experts. And every item she bought herself, the clothing, the kitchen ware, the beautiful bedding, the towels that would be super soft, she would have sent to the new address. She would buy one of the new electric cars and have that stored in the garage beneath the apartments. And when all that was complete, she would leave him.

Within a few weeks, she had accomplished most of what was on her list. It wasn't hard to do. She just sat on her new computer stored carefully at her work place. Every lunch break and before she left for home, she would place another three or four orders. She decided she would leave him with all her old clothes, the old bed sheets, the well-used crockery and cutlery. Even the pantry she would leave full, full of the items she preferred and he detested. She enjoyed imagining the challenge he would face. She would take nothing. Just walk out the door. At the new apartment, she would shower and change her clothes. She would choose what matched and what made her look so much prettier than the fifty-year-old, slightly gaunt figure she was now.

Then she would order to be delivered all the food she thought she would like to try. The pantry would be stocked to the brim; cupboards would hold only new gleaming crockery. Every drawer would be filled with beautiful cutlery. And she would have a few dozen bottles of champagne sent from the most expensive liquor store in town.

She had already spoken to the Concierge at the Apartments who knew to open her apartment, the one she had bought that overlooked the lake, and who for a negotiated retainer was carefully putting every item she had ordered into the apartment for her. She trusted him; money talked and she was generous towards him. After all, she knew what it was like to value every penny. His eyes would light up at the extra tip she left with him. And he knew to be discrete.

At the end of the four weeks, she knew she was ready. She returned home at the end of the working day, put her husband's meal into the oven, set the table, and waited.

He wolfed down his meal without a word of thanks. Knocked the head off a beer and settled down on the sofa with the newspaper. She waited until he was settled and then told him she was leaving him. The taxi tooted at the front door as he registered that she actually meant what she said. He scoffed at her, derided her for her thoughts that she could manage anything without him. She gave him a half smile as he said she'd be back just as soon as she realised that, without his pay packet, she would never manage. And picking up her well-worn handbag she walked through the front door to the waiting taxi.

She left.

The next day, to her supervisor's surprise, she handed in her notice. He shook his head, privately thinking she'd likely end up on the streets. No husband, no job.

In quick succession, she changed her name, bought a new phone, and had a passport created for her. She settled into her apartment and, armed with travel pamphlets, she began the next phase of her life.

The old phone rang incessantly as her husband tried to make contact with her; she just turned the sound off and counted the number of calls he made each day. She spent her time in the travel agents, or the beauty parlour, or learning how to use her new TV set, or her new musical technology. She enrolled in piano lessons, and a book club, and went to lectures on all manner of subjects as she prepared to take a holiday voyage on the *Three Queens* to parts of the world she had only ever heard about.

She planned that carefully so that she would be away from her apartment for about six months. *That should do it*, she thought. *How to become a new me in six wonderful months.* And that made her laugh, the first laugh she'd had in years. Then she thought maybe holidaying six months of every year would be an option, too, and she laughed even harder.

It wasn't until she had been around the world and had made a variety of new friends in a class she hadn't known existed that she accidentally bumped into her husband. Long since divorced, he had a new woman in tow. And she looked at her and sighed. There was a replica of herself. Down at heel, dowdy clothes, not much spare flesh on her, hair going grey, exactly as she had been. He didn't recognize her at first, and when he did and saw the smartly dressed, beautifully coiffured woman who stood tall and proud before him, his face crumbled. She held his eye and spoke in her new and cultured voice, politely and with perfect diction. She glanced at his new partner and then moved away. He was speechless.

How easy it had been, she reflected, to become the woman she had always wanted to be. Her talent in recreating herself had been her gift. And she enjoyed the fact that she had done it all without him realising he had been entitled to half of the fortune she had won.

❧

The Traveller

It had always been a dream of hers, to travel.

Oh, to visit distant places, to see different people, to try their food, see their customs, and engage with people she had only ever read about. Her eyes lit up with the joy her thoughts brought her.

She smiled at her fantasies of the Himalayas and the people who lived in Nepal. Not rich or wealthy like so many Western countries, but they seemed to be so rich in their culture and their people. How they worked so hard and made so much of the little they had. Weather-beaten skins and faces that never told their age, their lives centred around their families.

Her thoughts floated to other family-oriented countries. She thought of the people who lived on islands in the Pacific and how they were always portrayed as happy people. They loved their food and their rugby, and they seemed to create festivities for all sorts of reasons.

If the crops grew well, or a beautiful baby was born, they celebrated. How they enjoyed themselves, the fun they created. She knew of the Fijians' love of singing and how their churches rang out with religious song.

She knew, too, how their culture was patriarchal. Property was passed down through the men in the family. And as she thought about that she wondered how many other cultures were like that. She knew, too, how the Polynesians loved their food, their ovens in the ground. But she wasn't sure that they used many spices, and she wondered why? Did their countries not grow spices?

And her mind slipped into thinking about the countries that did use spices in their food. Indian cultures, their love of spice, the aromas they could create when cooking. She could almost smell the hot curries she had tried in the past. Indeed, she had tasted many a curry from the Curry House in her small town.

But she had never been to India, nor would she ever go to the Pacific, nor would she ever watch a game of rugby again.

She had wanted to feel snow, too; well, you can't play Rugby in the snow, can you? But just once, she would have liked to watch the snowdrops fall, to watch the snow mount up until you could make snowballs and engage in playfulness with children and adults while making a snowman. She chuckled as she thought of the carrot they always used for the snowman's nose, then sighed, she had never decorated a snowman.

That was never going to be a possibility for her.

She lay in her bed and let her mind wander like a magic carpet from country to country. She often opened her large Atlas and would spend hours imagining what it would be like to ask to go to another country and actually be taken there! To be immersed in their activities, to try their food, and to wear their clothes.

Her mind's eye saw the photos of the gold jewellery that the Jeweller's shops displayed in some of the Asian countries. So beautiful. But then her face clouded over – not for her an arm full of golden bracelets, or the glorious golden hooped earrings.

But she brightened as she thought how wonderful it must be to be driven across desert sands, watching a sunset over hills of sands, then to crowd into a tent and sit cross-legged while sharing food with your fellow travellers. Now that would be her idea of heaven. She would learn, she really would, how to scoop up food with the flatbreads they served, no knives and forks, just clever use of the breads they made. She longed to touch the silks the women wore and to find how they kept them all in place while they worked. She often thought she would be hopeless at that; the silk would just slither off her, she felt sure of it.

Her mind darted here and there. She wondered what it would be like to sit in a Paris coffee shop while having her breakfast, and being so Parisian reading the newspapers while she drank her coffee so slowly. And then she thought, *but I can't even speak French let alone read it.* And the ghost of a smile played across her face.

She had read quite a lot of history over the years and could be quite creative when she thought of the Roman days, the Roman people, although she imagined that they were now very like the Parisians, beautifully dressed, with exquisite bags and accessories. She liked their food, the pasta, and the meatballs, but she knew nothing in the world compared to French cooking. The sauces, the meats, the flavours. Oh, how magical it would be to sit in a Michelin restaurant and just order whatever took her fancy. To have a chef who would cook everything just the way she liked it. And serve it to her himself. Why were chefs always men? Now she knew that in today's world, that wasn't so anymore, but she was kind of stuck in yesteryear thinking. Her imagination always conjured up male chefs. *Oh girl,* she said to herself, *you are showing your age.*

She lay for a little while, her mind almost empty. She had travelled far and wide today; she had used her imagination to its limit, even without the Atlas or her library of History books for help.

And so, she let her mind see the sea, and the small boat that took her out onto the calm waters and let her drift. She had the blue sky for company, the stillness only broken by the gentle lap-lap of the water against the hull of the boat. She snuggled into her pillows and let the imagined sun's rays warm her as she closed her eyes.

Today was a beautiful day, she had travelled all around the globe; she had created lovely thoughts; she had seen caring people and watched customs that made her smile, and now she was tired.

And she let sleep take her, as the nursing staff by her bedside tucked her blankets in and quietly tiptoed out of her hospital room to leave her to take her rest.

Ↄ

The Waiting Room

She sits quietly waiting her turn to see the doctor. The surgery seems busy; people come and go. With six doctors in the Centre, it seems like the flotsam and jetsam of life pass through these doors. She searches the parade looking for characters she might use in her new book. She's always on the lookout for faces and figures and distinctive traits that she can write around her characters.

Take that man sitting alone in the corner. His head down, his hands speak of helplessness as they clasp and unclasp while he waits. Amazing how a figure can portray dismay and distress so clearly. The word that had sprung into her mind was forlorn. He looks poor but that's because his clothes depict a lack of care. And her fertile mind wondered if he once had a wife or a someone who attended to such basic needs, and perhaps now he no longer had that help.

Then there was the frazzled woman sitting a few seats from her. Her active imagination set the story around her. A mother, little time for herself, needing to rush in an appointment before the children finished school for the day.

And then the elderly couple quietly sitting opposite her. Neither speaking. With all the time in the world to wait, patiently. Who was the patient, she wondered, and who was there for moral support? Or perhaps, who was the one who would remember the doctor's words after they got home.

They were tidily dressed, each with a small bag beside them. A man bag for him and a handbag for her, and she wondered if you emptied the contents of each bag what they would contain. In his would be his glasses, his wallet, some cards, and the always present Bus pass that allowed him to use the bus services free during the day. In hers would be a purse containing her cards, all manner of items for "just in case" they were needed. The obligatory tissues, perhaps gloves, receipts, a notebook and pen, and the cosmetics she used.

Her name was called. She decided she would take herself off to the Bakery Café after her appointment was finished. She wanted to continue the people survey she had started. All people gave her information she could use – the hats they wore, which depicted their era – the handbags, large or small, which indicated their life style – the shoes they wore, which complimented their outfit, or decidedly did not, but rather spoke of stepping into anything that would get them out the door in a hurry. Were they scuffed, or tidy but not cleaned often, or on the rare occasion did they shine with the attention they had been given? Now those types of shoes interested her.

Her gaze shifted to the young man drinking his coffee a few tables from her. His shoes shone. They were not new, but they complimented the suit he was wearing. Everything about him exuded confidence. His hair, cut in a modern style, his suit tailored to fit his slim figure, and then there were his nails. Perhaps he used a manicurist? They were neat and uniform. His tie was the only thing that looked a little out of place. His neat blue shirt was decorated with a rather ugly tie, sort of grey with deeper grey swirls. *Mmm*, she thought, *a present, or a lack of dress or colour sense.* She decided he had no colour sense; that satisfied her wandering mind as she settled her gaze on the newest person to enter the café.

The man had long blonde hair tied back with a band of some sort. His white shirt rippled with the muscles it constrained. His beige trousers and loafer shoes depicted a man of some consequence, someone who knew his attractiveness and wore it well. After a while, she placed the face. She had seen it in the newspaper during the week. She remembered the photo of him as he walked from the Supreme Court with his lawyer, ignoring photographers, and walking towards a waiting car. He had been set free after answering charges of Insider trading. The evidence had been insufficient to convict him. The judge had ruled it that way, which seemed to her to be a way of saying, 'well, this time you got away with it.'

Her attention now completely caught, she took a sip of her almost cold coffee and she watched him walk to the table of the young man with the shining shoes and ghastly tie. They greeted each other warmly and he sat down. Their conversation was animated, and satisfied. How did she know that? It was all in their body language: they glowed, their eyes danced, their hands on the table were gesticulating and happy. Yes, your hands can reflect happiness.

She studied them intently, her active mind formulating her storyline. She knew she would have to research Insider trading, but she had her characters. They both sat at the table next to the door. They had successfully made millions through some clever Insider trading. And while they would enjoy their wealth, something about them both made her think they got away with it this time, and because they were young and their egos large, they would try it again. And this next time they would not be so lucky. Of this, she was sure. And, certainly, her book would develop how they would allow themselves to get duped by their early success and make the greatest of mistakes by trying to repeat their actions. The Financial Watchdogs were those with long memories and a penchant for watching patterns on the stock markets of the world.

And really, she would be writing fiction, but based on the intuitiveness of a good writer and her instinct for taking real-life characters and creating a story around them. She had all the food for her creativity from her morning's outing. She mused about today's characters as she slowly walked home thinking of how she would weave them into her book, and she smiled as she thought of the elderly couple in the waiting room. They would be the heroes of her story. She wasn't sure yet how they could unmask insider trading but a little bit of research would give her the answers. She would give them time and intelligence and, yes, persistence, and how would her youthful readers respond to that? With horror. Now she chuckled. She knew the older readers would love it all.

With the opening lines to Chapter One flying around in her head, she walked up her driveway, anxious to get the growing thoughts down on paper.

Her waiting room observations had formulated her dominant characters, and her coffee break had formulated the story. It had been a good day out.

❧

The Wedding

She had this dream that she would walk down the aisle on her father's arm and that her husband-to-be would be waiting for her at the altar with a smile that lit up the room. In her dream, she had all her family and friends waiting to hear her pronounce her vows and to shower her with rose petals, so much nicer than confetti. The gaiety, the laughter, the fun, and the memories they would create.

But the dream would forever be just that, a dream. Because that is not what happened.

She worked as a vet at the Sydney Zoo, and her husband-to-be was a "suit". Well, that's what they called everyone who worked in an office, all the white-collar workers nowadays were called "suits". A junior partner in a law firm, he was just finding his feet. Who to take advice from, who to make sure he was on the right side of, who was who in the firm, and how much weight his voice carried. Not much, he told her often. But he was a fast learner and she knew he would make the most of his opportunities.

She, on the other hand, had been at the zoo for the last five years. Almost a veteran. And that in itself caused problems. Some of the more difficult cases landed on her doorstep or, more literally, on her operating table. She had become adept at wielding the scalpel, and there were numerous animals in the zoo that owed their lives to her. She had the ability to read an animal's pain, locate its origin, and make quick decisions. She was worth the rise they had given her, the appreciation they showed her. And that veterinary skill actually became her undoing on the day of their wedding.

Everything was planned: a day of beautification, hair, nails, and even a massage before donning THE wedding gown. The gown was old and vintage looking which looked ethereal on her, transforming her into a beauty stepping from the pages of the past. In truth, it had been her grandmother's, and she had loved every inch of the lace that fitted her slight frame; she knew her grandmother was looking down and enjoying the reuse of her dress. Theirs had been a bond of the young and the old with stories and history shared. Now she was about to take that history into her own life.

But, and there is always a but, isn't there.

On the morning of her wedding, as she settled back in her apartment and the hair dresser worked miracles with her long hair, winding it around her head and filling it with tiny roses as she talked to her bridesmaids, and watched as they opened a bottle of bubbling champagne, her mobile phone rang. She picked it up, expecting it to be a call from Mark, her husband-to-be. But no, it was from the zoo.

The drama unfolded. Lily, the zoo's most precious elephant was in labour, and that labour had turned into trauma. The baby was stuck in the delivery passage. The hours were passing. The elephant had become distressed, and as they monitored her it had become apparent that she was going to need extra assistance. Please could she help? And yes, of course, they had tried to get other veterinary assistance but no one was prepared to operate on Lily. No one felt competent to deal with the unknown, and if it came to the anesthetising of an elephant and the caesarean operation on an animal that size, and that weight, and how could they keep her from crushing the baby, and … and … and … there were so many reasons given. She understood.

Do I get married or do I deliver a baby elephant? It was as simple as that.

So Mark received a phone call while Sandra donned her working clothes and her bridesmaids looked on in horror.

"You'll have to explain to everyone for me," she said. "I just haven't got time. As soon as I am able, I'll get to the church. Perhaps you could take my wedding gown there, and I'll change at the church. Please, please tell everyone to wait for me. I reckon it will take me about two hours from now, and I want you to send the taxi for me two hours from now. Please," she said again. And they all nodded, noticing how incongruous it was to see the flowered head in the khaki work gear depart from the house.

Well, Sandra's mop cap hid the flowers and kept the shape of the beautiful coiffure, and her operating clothes covered her newly massaged form, her mask covered the makeup so exquisitely applied, and the gloves preserved the lacquered nails as she set about the task of assisting Lily to deliver.

No mean task. The anaesthetic could not be long lasting so she had to be quick. The elephant needed to be up on her feet as soon as the baby was delivered. She decided against a caesarean, thought she would lose both animals that way; instead, she donned the equipment needed to rotate the baby elephant and wondered if her arm would survive the contractions. With every contraction, she withdrew her arm and then, after it was over, plunged deeper into Lily and tugged and turned the baby. Four times, she did this while the staff looked on, until finally, she said, "She's moving again. I think she's coming through."

Two hours from the start to the finish, and Lily was standing looking with pride at her achievement. And the staff cheered and whooped with delight at the tragedy that had been averted.

Sandra looked at herself and decided it was definitely going to be a day she would remember.

As she walked out tired but happy, her arm incredibly sore and her roses a little wilted from their endeavors, she was met by her chief bridesmaid.

Nothing daunted the bridesmaids; they had brought the mountain to Mohammed.

There, in the lecture theatre at the zoo, were her parents, and the entire group of friends invited to the wedding. They whisked Sandra into a side room and began to dress her, powdered her nose; put another couple of pins in her hair. Looked for her shoes and realised they had forgotten them. "Sod the shoes," they all cried. "Boots will do."

And so it was that the zoo had a wedding and a baby delivery on the same day. The minister had obligingly driven to the zoo with the husband-to-be, and all the cars along the entranceway blocked the visitor's entrance while the wedding took place. Nothing was going to stop this day from being extra special, and they would collect the shoes on the way to the reception.

It was the worst of times and the best of times, and a day that the staff of the zoo, and the invitees to a wedding would never forget. The photos were taken with the boots on, and later with the wedding slippers on. The wedding at the zoo was recorded, made the news and the front page of the paper the following day. The bridesmaids told everyone that their plan was to see Sandra married in her dress, or her scrubs, depending on how long the delivery took. And the invitees had agreed that their unexpected trip to the zoo was another highlight of the day. And the newly married couple didn't let on that the bride was too exhausted to do anything except sleep the night away in the very expensive hotel booked for the wedding night. Not to mention she could hardly move her right arm for days afterwards.

CR

Through the Eyes of a Child

My Mean Mother

Why was I born to such a mean mother? She really didn't like me getting on the horse bareback. Now I don't know why she worried about that. They were racehorses, but a horse is a horse, isn't it? And they were meant to be ridden.

She didn't like me climbing the trees. Well, I suppose getting stuck up a few trees and having to be rescued was probably a bit of a trial for her. But hey, being stuck up high and not being able to find footholds to get back down was really quite scary.

And I hid my clothes after falling into the stream; I just don't know how she found them and washed them and put them back in my drawers. Not that that stopped me from trying to swing over the stream again, or paddle in the water that raced along.

And why did she growl when I went for long bike rides with my girlfriend? We took apples and fruit and biked forever. It was sort of dark when we turned to come home. But we made it and she growled.

And why did my mean mother cut down her old dresses and make them into dresses for me? I didn't even like dresses. I much preferred the shorts my brothers wore.

I know she worked hard on her knitting machine, making clothes to sell in the shops, but why didn't she make some of them for me. I tell you, I had a mean mother.

And why did she make me eat the food she put in front of

me? I didn't like vegetable soup. I wanted creamy tomato soup, and chops and sausages. And she made me eat so many vegetables just because she grew them in the garden.

And the raspberries she grew: I had to wait until she wasn't looking to dive into the vines and get an extra handful because she sort of rationed them out. But I fixed her. I climbed into the Mulberry tree, and you should have seen the mess I got myself into eating the juicy mulberries by the handful.

But the meanest trick of all was when she baked. She had three tins. One was mine and the others were for my brothers. She put biscuits and cake into each of the three tins, and that was it for the week. If you ate them all in just a day or two, my mean mother never put any more biscuits into the tins.

And my mean mother made me feed the lambs and the chickens. Well, I liked feeding the lambs, and I could laugh at my brothers milking the house cow, while my mother collected cream and made butter. But the chickens ... well, that was something else. Big buckets! And I was only a small girl. Was there ever such a mean mother?

The only time she wasn't so mean was when I got sick, which I did a couple of times. Then she put me into her big bed, where I could see out of her window into the orchard, and hear the birds, and watch the animals. And I could stay there all day. And she taught me to play cards, and would sit on the bed playing cards by the hour. And if it wasn't cards, I could play with her wedding dress, which was cream velvet. And I could wear it with her gold shoes, as a treat.

But the absolute height of meanness came when I was to go to Secondary School. My mean mother sent me to Boarding School. She said something about giving me some girls to play with. Well, I was quite happy with all the boys my brothers brought around. I could kick a football, and I was always a great boundary catcher in cricket. I know I got in their way quite a bit but I could match it with the boys any day of the week. And Boarding school was so far away.

At school, I had to write home every week – those were the rules. So, I told my mean mother about sneaking into the Nuns' kitchen and getting food for the girls in the dormitory. And the pillow fights, and the Sunday walks like a long snake of girls. Horrible. In our hats, suits and Lyle stockings. I had to mend every hole in those stockings because my mean mother wouldn't get me any more. They were all mend and no stocking by the time a year was up.

And she didn't visit me, because she was so far away. Now that was very mean. I went home for the holidays, and so much changed in that time. My brothers grew up, and my mean mother had another baby girl. And I thought my sister was beautiful, but I did worry that my mean mother mightn't let her play in the stream, or climb the trees, or feed the lambs as I did.

So you see, through the eyes of a child, the world is a very small place. It is what surrounds that child. It is every little escapade, every warm and toasty fire, every meat and three veg meal, every mad game of football, and every game of cards that a mother stops to play with her daughter.

CR

You Will Not Know the Hour or the Day for Whom the Bell Tolls

The day was darkening. Clouds loomed, threatening.

The winter winds blew resistance out of the walkers; the bike riders had long given up and returned to their homes; the car drivers had made the most of an early departure from work. The working day was winding down amidst the threatening advance of the storm.

But not all of the city's workers had their workday finished.

For some, it was just the beginning.

The Nursing staff changed shifts; the medical staff allowed the residents to take over the evening load; the cleaners emerged, buildings to clean, waste to be emptied, and the restaurateurs geared up for the evening's dinner, hopeful of some patrons.

And in among them walked the shadow of death.

To look at him, he was slight, dressed in unassuming clothing, nondescript in looks, but with a purpose in his step.

He, too, had a job to do. He, too, had a time frame and a purpose to his movements.

He hailed a cab to take himself out of the winds and the commencing rain. He gave the address and sat and waited. His eyes never reached those of the cab driver. His conversation was non-existent. He paid in cash, the benefits of still having cash as a commodity in this city.

He had work to do.

His surveying of the building earlier that week meant he knew which corners to turn, which doors to open and which staircase to take as he pulled his sleek leather gloves from his pocket.

His only indulgence was these expensive, beautifully crafted leather gloves, which he admired as he put them on.

There were no fingerprints on the door handles; nothing he touched would leave a mark incriminating him.

He took the lift to the 7th floor and emerged onto a carpeted floor as he walked to Flat 10.

He knocked, offering the mail he had collected earlier from her box. "Delivered into his box by mistake," he said.

She opened the door to receive it. And that was all he needed.

He felt no remorse. He didn't know the woman; he just did his job.

The pay was good, and the demand was spasmodic but certainly never-ending.

In a city this size, there were jealous husbands, thwarted lovers, business partners, and those with an unsatisfied grudge, all willing to pay for their personal retribution to whoever had caused their ire.

The retribution may have been extreme, but he had no qualms about that. His involvement was only a cash contract which was paid before and after.

His word was his bond, and those who made use of his services were not those who needed to fear him. He could be reached only by those for whom he had performed a service, so they were unlikely to give him up to the law.

He walked away, another job finished. Another sum of money paid into his Moroccan account. Someone else now marked off his list. He still had two more names to account for before the end of the month. Then he planned on a retreat to his small beach house to fish.

He crossed the road and took the path through the park towards the taxi stand on the opposite side of the park.

His mind was empty of thoughts, his footsteps as deliberate as his personality and as he walked the crack sound only penetrated his consciousness slightly, above the noise of the wind and now heavy rain.

He couldn't avoid it as the huge branch self-pruned from the fig tree fell, and crushed him.

In an effort to give him a name, the police traced this through the expensive gloves he had in his pockets.

And the residue of blood on the gloves traced to the death of the young woman in Block Twenty, Floor 7, Flat number 10.

And Lucifer rubbed his hands together with glee as he welcomed the latest inhabitant to hell.

And neither had known the hour or the day.

CR

Your Honour

I put pen to paper to explain to you, your Honour.

Why I am standing here in court, your Honour;

It's not because he took my money, your Honour;

Or went with other women, your Honour;

It's not because he was caught wildly betting on the horses, your Honour;

Or even because the TV remote is stuck on sport, your Honour.

I plead guilty, your Honour.

I did it.

I took his bike and trashed it.

Look, your Honour, you have to see it from my perspective:

If he rides twenty kilometres each day, this is the outcome:

7 pot holes, Main Roads are so incompetent!

3 dangerous roundabouts, who designed this madness …

4 inexperienced L platers, shouldn't let them get behind the wheel!

6 wayward pedestrians, keep to the left, don't cha know the rules,

1 he shouldn't-have-his-licence-bus driver, no road sense,

5 taxi's, deliberately going slow,

10 dogs-out-roaming, without their owners,

7 posties, in his pathway,

11 mothers, pushing strollers,

20 grannies on pushers, – blind as bats,

6 tree roots, on the pathway,

2 roads, without footpaths,

5 Hot riders, without a bell,

3 sprinklers, left turned on,

4 hedges, needing a haircut,

12 grandpas on motorised ride-ons – without their hearing aides in,

8 children, doing wheelies on the way to school.

And 3 magpies, swooping on his helmet!

Not to mention the flock that pooped on his bike in the park,

You see, your Honour?

Thank you for understanding, your Honour.

Yes, I'll take the suspended sentence, your Honour.

And no, sir, you won't see me again.

Now, come on, Graeme, it's time to walk me home.

❧

Tiny Tales at Christmas time

Christmas
Comes.
Hustle and Bustle.
Clean up happens
Normal again.

Food. Glorious food.
Table spread
With joy
Consumed
With love.

Christmas
Never alone
Always friends
Sharing
Champagne Song
And laughter.

Christmas
With family
With friends
With joy
With love
Together.

❧

Christmas Time

She unwraps her gifts
Slowly
She reads the cards
Carefully
She smiles with dimples
Gracefully
She speaks her thanks
Sincerely
She is filled with wonder
Happily.

A little girl at
Christmas time.

&

Dear Grandmother

You lived such a short life, and you never knew me, but I feel like I have always known you through my grandfather. He told us so many stories about you. He had known you since school days and he says he loved you from the first moment he saw you. I was born in 2080 when my mother, your daughter, was thirty.

You died in the second worldwide pandemic of coronavirus, which everyone called the X virus. That was in 2055 when my mother was five. So many people died, generations of humans. No country was immune from the enormous toll of human life lost. It was the first time in history that the World Health Organisation seconded the scientists in the world to work together to find a way to vaccinate against the X virus and then find a cure. They shared laboratories and ideas and came together in a magnificent way. It was either that or the world would have perished.

And, Grandmother, I want to tell you how they found the cure. They used Artificial Intelligence, or AI, to help humans. AI is simply technology that simulates human intelligence. With the input of so much intelligence into one central point, first the vaccination was found, and then the cure. We will never have another viral pandemic like that again because we have found the cause, how it spreads, and a cure for it. And this all happened with the use of AI.

I am looking back, Grandmother, to the time when you lived as a young woman, back when there was no complete cure for

Cancer or cure for Alzheimer's disease.

I want to tell you that we have a cure for both of these diseases now. I am only twenty and this year, the year 2100, is a magnificent year for medical discoveries brought about by our Medical Research Centres. Grandmother, the world has gone from strength to strength, all with the help of AI.

We have been feeding so much information into our AI machines in the Research Fields. This has allowed us to finally detect the way Cancer cells mutate and from a simple test we can now prevent its growth. Cancer was the leading cause of death before the Virus X.

I have so much that I want to tell you, because so much has happened in the second half of the century just passed, so much that you would be glad of.

The Cancer research was a collaborative affair between several countries. This automatically followed on after the cure for Virus X. You would have marvelled at the information that was shared. Somehow, differences were put aside by the world's top scientists, and they all worked together. The Nobel Prize for Medicine, 2080, was awarded to the group of Australian medical scientists who were able to prevent the growth of Cancer; the World applauded them and Australia was so proud of their work.

That didn't happen with Alzheimer's disease. With Alzheimer's disease, the pharmaceutical companies have been fighting each other for years. They are all trying to gain control of the right to produce medication that cures Alzheimer's. The medication removes the plaque that causes it. We knew about plaque when you were alive but what made the difference was AI found the chemicals that dissolve all plaque. Even the Early Onset Alzheimer's disease can now be stopped in its tracks. It is a miracle that we all owe to AI.

We all use AI now, but in a way that you would approve of. Sort of like a personal assistant. And, Grandmother, the most amazing thing has happened. AI itself has been used to prevent AI from being used in a criminal way against humans. Research Scientists used AI's powers to show us how to *stop* AI from being used against humans. No one has been able to crack the code AI created for this.

For years we were all scared AI would be able to turn on humans. Now we all use it in so many helpful ways. You would smile to see AI teaching all the grandparents how to use AI. I do so wish you were amongst those older people; I want to know what you would have used it for.

One of the crazy things AI has done is stop the Peanut allergy in the Western World. AI found the allergen in the peanut oil and removed it. Remember the Epi-pens children carried with them in case of a reaction to peanuts? That has gone now.

AI is controlling the financial status of our country, and our banks use AI to prevent the scamming that happened for so many years. Your sister told me about the time you were scammed when buying very expensive Theatre Tickets. Those scams have long gone. Of course, humans will always commit crimes against one another, but that is a feature that we are working on right now, security. I think that my children's generation will eventually grow up in a much safer world.

AI is now able to detect guns so the police force is slowly ridding us of these weapons, and the production of guns is severely restricted. Other countries are taking our lead, and one day, perhaps in my lifetime, with the reduction in weapons, we may put a stop to wars. The future depends on how confrontations and disagreements can be resolved without weapons. I don't know the role AI will play in this but our scientists are deeply involved in this right now.

Because AI has shown so many countries the profitable crops they can use to replace drug crops, our world is moving towards a better human life. Those countries where poverty was extreme are now able to grow fast crops and eat healthily. The drug scene is waning, and with it, crime rates are declining. So many governments have now banned drug crops, AI can detect them, and the Fireys burn them.

You have seen I have written how AI is used to detect products that cause us harm. That came about through the scientific investigations into smell. Animals taught us this, and AI has used how their senses work to create detectors that we can use.

Our medical teams are now working in third-world countries to improve their health. So, along with AI's development of nutritious crops, there is also the control of diseases. Vaccinations have wiped out so many diseases since they were introduced to third-world countries. AI was responsible for the rapid development of multi-disease vaccinations, so of course, we all need fewer shots because of that.

The most interesting thing AI has been used for is job creation. AI created jobs we didn't even know we needed. Much of that is related to space travel and it is predicted that living on the moon will be a reality this century. Imagine going to the moon as though it were a Sunday drive. There are rare minerals on the moon that will be able to be used to create new medicines. Testing of samples by AI has already shown that medical breakthroughs are pending. That is so exciting, Grandmother. What other diseases do you think will become a thing of the past?

Our world population has slowed in growth as AI has shown us clever ways to produce food and not children. Food is very different to what you knew but it is tasty and healthy. We are learning to make it look good as well as taste great. We now have vegetable crops that are hybrid, using the stronger crops but growing them like the prolific wheat crops. And they are all disease free.

We still love our animal food, but animals no longer contribute to climate change. When seaweed was discovered to reduce the methane gas animals produced AI was used to create grasses that contain the same preventative product as the seaweed. It created an industrial storm. Companies invested money into these grasses and, in turn, thousands of jobs were created. We still use the seaweed to give variety to animal diets and that has meant Seaweed Farms have proliferated and now rival Fish Farms in number.

And Fish Farms, Grandmother, we have them everywhere. AI has taught us how to be productive with this. Mother has shown me pictures of the crayfish Christmas Dinners you loved to have. Well, it is now an everyday food. Our diets have improved with the balance of foods we eat nowadays, and nutritionists think we will live much longer than the generations before us.

While you were alive, Seaweed scientists began using seaweed to replace plastic. That was another huge industry growth that occurred after Virus X was controlled. We all use what looks like plastic and even feels like plastic, yet it is biodegradable. All seaweeds can be used, and this has given less wealthy countries a product that is marketable worldwide.

The world population has slowed, as I told you. That's due to education in Third World Countries. Here AI has played a huge role. We make programmes in all languages that can be shown in even the poorest of homes with no electricity. We finally found how to store energy simply, and that has enabled the Teaching Tablets, another AI invention, to work together with Teachers in education. Children are helping to teach their parents. Homework is something shared by families, and understanding the new technology in growing crops is increasing at a level even I find amazing. Of course, self-regulation in reducing population is not easy, but once again, the scientists are being creative and with the help of AI they are using education about family size, making it manageable for us all. I think originally, AI wanted something to be added to the water we drink to control the population, but that got overruled.

Grandmother, the biggest favour AI has done is to create a need for scientists, and that is what I am studying now at the Scientist University of WA. You see, there is such a great need for scientists that a new university is being built as I write. This is the university I have been attending for the last two years. You would be proud of me. I finish this year. My degree, when I have completed it, will be a Bachelor of Scientific Intelligence, and that's just a basic degree. The university is scrambling to provide enough teachers for the higher degrees but that will happen. Or maybe the teachers will be robots!

I have written this letter to you as a part of my studies. My student group has created a Time Capsule which will be opened at the university in 2200. We hope the students will be able to see the changes in our society through our eyes, and perhaps they can create a similar picture for the year 2300 science students. It would be fascinating for it to continue.

I think AI began to be used so much more when the Mining Giants turned to it. That was back in the 2020s. They had the money to make AI grow. Everything seemed to start around that time, but when the Mining firms allowed their knowledge to be used, that changed everything. That, in turn, created scientists who took the new information into crops, medicine, cars, and every field imaginable.

Remember how your generation always laughed at cars being able to drive themselves? And all your life people were trying to make this happen? Well, it has finally become a reality. It did take a long time for sensors and car programmes to be sufficiently safe for car users to buy into this market. And all the manufacturers played it safe. No one wanted claims against them, so it took much longer than expected. But alongside that is what is under investigation now – how to use the air-waves as road waves, and allow people to travel in their air pods.

This field has also taken time to become available for everyone. Government allowed the research but the scientists couldn't keep up with it. There was so much to learn. Now AI has grasped how to have sky highways it is going to be relatively simple to let people fly to work. The birds of the air will have to make way as humans fly with them. But how to teach birds airway rules? Well, that is beyond me.

I have saved the best for last. The worldwide reliance on fossil fuels has shifted. When the ability to store electricity was achieved, it lessened the dependency on fossil fuels. What you used to call the Petro Dollar is now a term no longer used. Fossil fuels are a commodity we still use but all cars are now electric. All homes now have smaller and more efficient solar panels, and also water tanks. That is compulsory. This means that each house can supply its own electricity and what is left over goes into the grid. The Gas and Coal industries have been transitioning remarkably well into products that will be used in space projects.

The world's drier countries are learning ways to find and retain water and that is an ongoing need for this century. Something the scientists are being creative about. We have to learn ways to make the water cycle work well in all countries, and that is what I will be working on into the future.

Dear Grandmother, this will be a new century, and a new world, with AI making lives so much happier. The things we dreaded about AI have not been allowed to become a reality. We are using it to benefit humankind and the potential into the future is much more than we could ever have imagined. I am now thinking that perhaps this is what our world was meant to look like, a place where we used all our knowledge for good. I do so wish you were here to share this new world with me.

Today I will add this letter to be kept in the time capsule and opened when the world turns 2,200. I feel a huge excitement in saying that.

In 100 years' time, will my grandchildren say, "This is how people lived back then?" Will they, too, have so much to be thankful for?

ख

Entrant in The Yarn Competition 2024 WA

About the Author

Lynley grew up in New Zealand but has spent most of her adult life in Australia.

Her working life saw her achieve three careers: first in General and Psychiatric Nursing, then teaching nurses, counselling, and finally, Mediation (An Alternative Dispute Resolution Practitioner, mentoring, teaching, and practising).

When Lynley retired from her job, she resumed her lifelong passion for writing.

She is encouraged by her husband, and four adult children without whose technical wizardry she would still be using pencil and paper.

She was once asked, "Where do you get your ideas from?" and said, "I see a story in everything. Show me anything, a word, a picture, a character, and I can make a story from it."

This is a collection of some of the short stories she has had the fun of creating. Enjoy the stories she has written.